Marina Reader

AUSTIN MACAULEY PUBLISHERS
LONDON * CAMBRIDGE * NEW YORK * SHARJAH

Copyright © Marina Reader 2025

The right of Marina Reader to be identified as author of this work has been asserted by the author in accordance with sections 77 and 78 of the Copyright, Designs and Patents Act 1988.

All rights reserved. No part of this publication may be reproduced, stored in a retrieval system, or transmitted in any form or by any means, electronic, mechanical, photocopying, recording, or otherwise, without the prior permission of the publishers.

Any person who commits any unauthorised act in relation to this publication may be liable to criminal prosecution and civil claims for damages.

This is a work of fiction. Names, characters, businesses, places, events, locales and incidents are either the products of the author's imagination or used in a fictitious manner. Any resemblance to actual persons, living or dead, or actual events is purely coincidental.

A CIP catalogue record for this title is available from the British Library.

ISBN 9781035880003 (Paperback)
ISBN 9781035880027 (ePub e-book)
ISBN 9781035880010 (Audiobook)

www.austinmacauley.com

First Published 2025
Austin Macauley Publishers Ltd®
1 Canada Square
Canary Wharf
London
E14 5AA

The author's widow is very thankful to Austin Macauley Publishers for the opportunity to take up the manuscript for sharing with readers.

Chapter 1
Number 24

Charlie glanced across the few intervening feet of office space to check on the rest of his staff, his personal assistant, his secretary, his assistant manager, and the office junior, she smiled back brightly. For Bridget was all these things rolled into one, she reminded him of a cross between his own first wife and a young Maureen O'Hara with her pale freckled complexion and deep red hair. Of Irish parentage, but born and bred in England, with no trace of an accent. Working together, they formed a closeness and friendship that was a pleasure. Charlie had occasional vague sexual desires towards her; he felt sometimes that she maybe ever reciprocated, but it had never had a chance or reason to develop further. He knew, that when they were separated by holiday, he really missed her; obviously, he was attracted to her, for she was young and lovely, but he admired her as a colleague more, and he relied on her completely.

    She was a practising Catholic and prone to be moody, after the failure of her virginity. She was 26 now and engaged to Padraig, three years her junior in age and a lifetime her junior in experience. She had settled for him after a great deal of confusion. She had been heavily involved with one of the company's 'fliers,' but had gone for safety and reliability rather than excitement. She had married for all the wrong reasons, primarily because she was pregnant, which was something her parents couldn't cope with. And then tragically, she lost the baby. The marriage died with it, and one day, she literally left her husband a dear Jordan letter and ran off with a former lover to Ireland; that hadn't worked either and as he had learnt her story bit by bit, Charlie had grown to care about her more and more.

She bought out in him all his instincts of protection, and what he thought of as his 'better' feelings. She played down her natural attractions, dressing plainly on purpose, but on one odd occasion, he had seen her made up; she had indeed been a knockout; she was his for the working day though, and together they had done quite well.

For the past three days, he had been interviewing people for the Sunday morning job that had been advertised up until then the two of them shared this responsibility, but Charlie had prevailed upon the powers to let him get someone new as part timer for this and two Saturday mornings a month. "I must be coming to the end of this bloody list," he said. She laughed and reminded him that the next one on the list was number 24, a Mrs Mia Canetor.

"What the hell is she?" He asked. "Chinese or something, why couldn't I have number 17, that tasty little raver with the leather miniskirt and sex appeal?"

"You know full well why not," Bridget replied, "Jordan came straight out of the back office and told you 'Not our sort of person I think'." And for this, the last but three remaining he had already decided on one or two that he intended to recommend, and by now was just gone through the motions.

Number 24 walked through the door, and quite literally took his breath away, there was just something about her that physically smote him, and he had read of such things happening, but never in his life experienced it himself. She wasn't beautiful in the accepted sense, small, very attractive indeed, and with lovely freshly permed blond shoulder-length hair, nicely made up with nothing fleshy about her. It was her self-projection that hit him hardest; he noticed first her sparkling intelligent eyes and her warm genuine small face itself was rather thin, and what he could see under her coat seemed to indicate that there wasn't really much of her anywhere; she was wearing a grey top coat with a metallic thread shining in it and a bright red scarf that contrasted it perfectly; she had a quality about her that was totally natural.

Charlie immediately slipped into top gear, turning on his best and most relaxing style. He was completely absorbed by her, talking to her carefully explaining what the actual job would be about, and asking her why she wanted it. Her answers that she had worked for Volvo and Dickens & Jones before being married satisfied him, she had a secretarial experience which the job wouldn't really need, and she had not worked for the past five years whilst she had her two children, and now wanted to get out of the house and do something interesting again. She admitted she had no actual experience of estate agency, but that she had enjoyed the buying and selling involvement of her own homes and wanted to learn as much about estate agents as she could.

She had a naturally attractive speaking voice, and her self-projection was excellent without being pushy. Charlie told her the usual line and said he would let her know as soon as possible. He and Bridget, together with Kat from the back office, discussed her and agreed that she was just what they were looking for. Charlie was delighted when All Mighty agreed to interview her, he knew it was a formality, just the boss being the boss. And when he rang Mrs Canetor back, her pleasure over the phone was infectious, the die was cast.

Chapter 2
In the Beginning

Charlie had two women in his life to care for. His widowed mother who was in her seventies, was a lady of old school and self-taught business woman who had built up the family firm from scratch, after her divorce from his father, back in the days when divorce was extremely difficult, she had made her own way for several years, bringing up her small boy with some help from her family, until she eventually met and fell in love with the man who became Charlie's step farther.

The extent of her love for Arthur as he was known, was deep and lasting. He was the only man in her life, and family when they decided to live together; at the time that they met, she was 32 and he was 50. He had been married for years to a woman he hated and had no life at all with, no children, he had a senior manager's position, but since his wife would not divorce him, he had her to keep so there was never enough money to make life easy, he was a difficult man, inflexible, and really quite selfish, and although he had taken Charlie under his wing, he was quite incapable of showing the boy any real affection.

Charlie was therefore brought up in an atmosphere of uncertainty, rows and sulks, and the main function usually seemed to be his mother defending him because of his own faults, real or imagined, against the efforts of his stepfather to make him into the image he desired.

Charlie's mother also had years of heartbreak with old Arthur. He would go off on golf breaks for two or three days at a time, leaving her and the boy alone in a lovely, but completely isolated cottage in the country, and in later life, they parted for several periods, the last of which was over a year, during which time she would come and stay with her son again. The family business, that she and Arthur built up from scratch eventually prospered. And on his 22nd birthday, much against the wishes of his stepfather, Charlie joined them. They became inextricably reliant upon each other, and in spite of frequent fallings out, they enjoyed a very good quality of life, that none of them would have expected to achieve alone.

And then one day, all this changed with the arrival of the second woman in Charlie's life. At the time she arrived to become secretary, Kat was 30, she had been married to a police officer since she was 18 and had three children. Her husband and she had grown apart over the years; he was a macho man in all respects, totally involved with his work, and with that, he saw it as a 'man's' life. His idea of a good night out with his wife was to take her to the police club, sit her in a corner with the other wives, and send drinks over to her at half-hour intervals, whilst he got drunk at the bar with his mates and was the life and sole of the party. Later, he would indulge in five minutes' worth of coupling, and as soon as he was satisfied, he would fall into a noise sleep.

As a father, he ruled by fear and his strength and size made him a formidable figure indeed. He had other worthwhile features as well, of course, but in the end, drinking ruined the marriage for both of them.

Kat was attractive, with a very good figure for a three-time mother, she had lost her virginity at 17 to her fiancée and then married Daniel, her husband without knowing any other men. She was a good, intelligent and willing worker, and Charlie took great pleasure in teaching her the business. He was engaged to his long-time girlfriend Tracey at the time, but she was an air hostess, away a lot on exotic trips, and he was left alone for most of the time and was leading the life of a successful bachelor. He had the outward trappings and material possessions important to a young man in his late twenties; a luxury flat, a good satisfying job as a partner and for his thirtieth birthday, his ultimate status symbol, an Aston Martin identical to Jordan Bonds. He knew he probably would marry Tracey eventually, but he was in no real hurry.

Kat had never had an affair of any kind at all, but the feeling between them grew, and one Christmas, they became lovers. Circumstances dictated that it could only be an occasional thing, although they saw each other every day; she couldn't or wouldn't leave Daniel, and meantime pressure was growing from Tracey to name the day or else. Charlie just didn't have the hardness to say no to her. He was scared to death that Daniel would eventually find out and literally kill him. And really, he felt the only actual thing he had with Kat, apart from their working together as a team, was the fact that his sex life with her was the most satisfying he had ever known; with Tracey it was good, but certainly not exciting. But with Kat, it was something else again.

With Tracey, he could travel the world, and how could he really say he was against the marriage, without ever trying it, in any event, he wasn't losing Kat, she would still be there every day, only the sexual satisfaction would be missing and how important was that to a relationship anyway. Certainly, to Charlie, it was not a matter of life and death, just something very nice and his way of showing his love to his partner was by wanting to give her satisfaction before taking his own. He had always believed that a woman's needs were more important than a man's in this respect, and since he didn't have looks or physique, the women who were attracted to him and who actually became part of his life, as averse to those just passed through it, stayed long and lasting friends years afterwards. They sensed that he really cared about them as persons and in fact, most of his close friends were women; some who he had never had physical contact with at all. And so, at the age of 32, Charlie plunged into matrimony, for the first time.

Chapter 3
The Travelling Man

He said a tearful and passionate farewell to that side of his feelings to Kat and he and Tracey commenced a lifestyle that was the envy of most and suited them down to the ground. She was a fabulous cook; he was an accomplished entertainer, and their home became a centre for friends from both sides. He loved the world travel; she took him to America for the first time. He discovered the sheer excitement of San Francisco; the street cards fascinated him, the harbour front of little Italy, with its fishing boats, and seafood restaurants captivated him; the warehouse conversions along the front, so cleverly done as apartments and shops filled him with the thought, that why couldn't the same be done in London. So many derelict period buildings just rotting away around Docklands. What a waste!

He loved the feel of Hollywood, all the films he had ever enjoyed, and the stars he had followed in sheer nostalgia of the old Universal Studios and the magic of Disneyland, it had all been pulling him towards it for years. The awesome place and tranquillity of Yellowstone Park with the giant sequoia trees, living things that had been growing for three thousand years, he just had to walk up and feel them; it was as if they had been waiting there forever just for this moment. The Grand Canyon at dusk, the smell of darkness, and her sheer fantastic depth with all its myriad colours, everything on earth that he had always imagined, and nothing that was in any way a disappointment, nothing except one sad thing—Tracey just couldn't share them with him.

It was as if he was alone in his enjoyment. She had seen most of these wonderful places before, but to her even for the first time, they were just interesting things. She had no feel for them, certainly not like he did. Charlie would dream one day of having someone who not only loved him but who would just know and equally enjoy all the ideas and thoughts and depth of feeling that he needed so much to share. And who he could give his own love to with all that was in him. Tracey could never even come close to this. She tried, but the more she tried in one direction, the wider the gap between them grew. In the three years that they were married, she took him to Hawaii, where the fresh greenness of the islands, totally unlike the real tropics, the majesty of diamond head volcano, the colonial buildings and the feel of the place all gave it so much more atmosphere than any other American state he had seen.

The brashness and the tattiness of Honolulu, the feeling of excitement to be just sun bathing on the famous Waikiki beach, and the sense of tragedy and waste standing on the bottom of the old Arizona battleship, sunk upside down in Pearl Harbour on the day of infamy, knowing it was an unopened tomb for over a thousand American sailors, to be there with dozens of Japanese tourists all clicking away with their cameras brought home to him the utter flutily of war.

In India, there was the feeling of timelessness, walking the same path to the Taj Mahal, that his own father had during the war, and his favourite uncle had trod in the great war before that, staying for the first time in the Taj Hotel in Bombay, a place he would return to later, stopping off deliberately just to repeat the experience, the old part fascinated him with its sheer luxury and opulence, the slow turning ceiling fans, the intricate ceiling carvings and cornices, the amazing sorrier by legion of uniformed flunkeys.

The mixing of Indian and European cultures personified by the morning-suited wine waiter, who complete with engraved silver gorge round his neck, served a bottle of Tiger beer in a silver ice bucket, explaining that it was an alcohol-less day, the palm court orchestra playing at the afternoon tea dance, dressed in blazers with regimented badges, old school ties, and the Ivor Novello song book, yet each musician as Asian as could be. The thronging hordes of beggars in the streets, performing their entire repertoire of acrobatics for a couple of rupees, sailing on vastly overloaded barge across tea coloured sea of Elephant Island, climbing two hundred old stone steps, which left his immaculately safari-suited Parisian companion looking like a sponge that needed winging out, taking in the explicitly sexual Hindu carvings and listening to the explanations of their most uncomfortable looking positions.

The sheer overwhelming teeming crowds of Hong Kong, with its wonderful bargains, buying a huge cane butterfly chair and shipping it home for less than half the price it would have cost anywhere else, crossing into Red China for the day rattling around in ex-London transport buses built back in the thirties, and dilapidated beyond all measure, but still going strong, fabulous Chinese meals in the famous floating restaurants, wandering around Singapore and dining in the historic Raffles hotels, drinking in the same long bar that his father spent so many hours in so many years before, ogling the beautiful fragile young girls along Boogie street, finding it impossible to believe they were all transvestites, thrilling to the excitement of Bangkok with its huge advertising boards everywhere, the clandestine but absolutely irresistible visits to the high class brothels not actually indulging, but enjoying fully all the other services, including a back manipulation that left him feeling he was walking on air, lazing under the palms in Penang, the most gorgeous setting anywhere in the world, floating in the turquoise waters, and having lobster thermidor for breakfast, taking rail journey from Nairobi to Mombasa, chugging through the forests all night in starched linen sheets, breakfasting in the mahogany panelled dining car, watching zebras and elephants grazing free, watching a thunderstorm at night over the jungle.

Drinking in his local pub one Friday lunchtime, looking at his watch and saying casually, "Must be off, lads, I am flying down to Rio." And then doing just that, nonstop to Brazil, and soaking in the sun on Ipanema Beach, which really was full of tall and tanned and young and lovely girls, walking in the jungle, coming across little clearings where the natives had left offerings, joss sticks, food, for their departed spirits, climbing to the base of Christos, the giant stature of Christ that dominated the city.

They would go to Brittany just for lunch and a stroll through the pine woods, to Majorca and Palma just for

Saturday night out, and once with Charlie acting as a member of the crew to Zurich for a Sunday lunchtime drink, but in spite of the glamour and interest in seeing and doing all these exciting things, the relationship just hasn't got any true depth.

Tracey loved Charlie all right, and for her, their sex life was full and active; for him, it was never as satisfying as if had been with Kat, and he found that he was performing without any real desire, she would help herself almost and although it was still satisfying for both of them, it naturally lacked any real passion. Her mother was the worst type of music hall joke mother-in-law. Her interference and her total influence over Tracey caused no end of rows, her wish to start a family was something Charlie found impossible to come to terms with; it would have been financially difficult, would have meant an end to all their travelling, which he still loved, and most important of all, it would have been a tie, which he knew he would never be able to break. His own mother was far from blameless; she had encouraged the marriage initially. She looked forward to having a daughter-in-law that she could be affectionate towards and share things with, but with Tracey, anything other than a distant 'by appointment' relationship was impossible, so instead she grew close to Kat in the office, causing even more natural resentment with Tracey.

Charlie remembered that on his actual wedding day, events occurred that could have ruined everything. When he had arrived first at the church, he had been confident, calm and completely sure he had made the original decision, and then he was finally, sitting down at the front, chatting to his best man and aware only of the noise of people arriving.

Glancing over his shoulder, he suddenly realised that the entire church was a sea of faces jammed on both sides of the aisle and they were all staring at him. His collapse was immediate panic raced through him and he became almost paralysed. By the time Tracey arrived, he had forgotten everything that had been rehearsed and it wasn't until she came to his side and took his shaking hand that he actually dared to look at her, the term radiant as bride was never truer than at that moment. She really was more beautiful than she had ever been before or ever was again. Her red hair was like polished copper and her pale skin and scattering of freckles set off her green eyes to perfection, she noticed immediately the nervous state he was in, and at that one time, the first and only time in their entire relationship, she was the leader and he followed humbly behind her.

He could never retain any memory of the actual ceremony, but when it came time to sign the registry in this lovely old Saxon country church, when all should have been harmony and happiness, the first jarring note of what was to come, emerged his new mother-in-law had always expressed a preference for Charlie's natural father Lucas. Arthur was much too willy an old bird to put up with her nonsense, and she knew he was more than a match for her, there was no animosity ever between the two men. But Arthur had quite naturally expected to witness the marriage certificate; Charlie at that time still retained his father's name and his mother-in-law felt that for Arthur to sign in his Charlie's mother's deed poll name would not look so good. So, without reference to anyone except perhaps Tracey, she had arranged to have Luca's sign instead; they both stepped forward at the same time only for her to show Arthur back again, and Charlie's stepfather may have been many things but shooshable.

Charlie by this time was still not really aware that anything was wrong, but the old man swore till his dying day that if it hadn't been arranged with Charlie's knowledge, he should have made a stand there and then, on the way to the reception. Arthur and Charlie's mother had an enormous row about it. Once again, she was defending Charlie against him which only exacerbated the matter further. In consequence, they were nearly an hour late arriving; the dragon lady in the meantime had lined up everyone in the receiving queue all in order of precedence. She flatly refused to let anyone in until Charlie's mother arrived, as the guests grew more restive, it finally dawned on Charlie just what was going on. The fact that he had imbibed a couple of stiff drinks helped as well, and he then took his stand in his usual stubborn, not-to-be-budged way, overruled his brand-new in-laws, who after all were only paying for the entire day, and personally started the proceedings; chaos, of course, reigned, not helped at all by the presence of a group of hippy friends, who though invited, had not signified acceptances, and were unknown to the bride's parents; duly attired in jeans, caftans and beads, they made just the sort of impact they made everywhere, hippies had been out of fashion for several years, but these were long-time close friends of Charlie's and he was really happy to see them.

In the swinging sixties, they had been inseparable and the free dope smoking, drug-induced times they had enjoyed had seemed the ultimate in relaxation then, to anguished cries from the dragon lady, "Oh god, they are wearing jeans."

Charlie replied, "Yes, but they are wearing their best ones." The whole affair developed into two separate receptions, with the bride and groom, and all their friends having a glorious champagne send-off drink at Gatwick Airport, and the respectful families retreating to their individual wedding night. Other than his determination to make it something very special for his bride to remember in the traditional way, years later, she told him it was everything she had ever anticipated for such an occasion, and that she did in fact hear bells ring four times; he often thought he wished he hadn't actually missed sharing that with her.

Chapter 4
All Change Here

Three years later, his stepfather Arthur died in hospital following surgery. Charlie was devastated; thrust into the only man's place, he was constantly surrounded by reminders of him and clients who hadn't heard would call and ask for him. His unfinished work all had to be completed, just as he had held it; his last appointments had to be carried out, and three weeks later after the funeral, he had died on Charlie's own birthday of all days, a particularly odious tenant called to the office.

The old man had originally done him a favour by letting him rent a flat, against his better judgment, but because he knew the family, years before, he was always in arrears and nothing but trouble. Cocky and rude, he strode into what had been the old man's office demanding to see that old bastard about a letter he had sent him, when told by a stunned Kat, that Arthur as in fact only recently died, he sneered and said about time too, stupid old fool.

Not another word was said, but in the only moment in his life when he had absolutely no control over himself at all, Charlie went for him like a mad bull, smashing aside his defending blows without even feeling them. He beat this creature to a facial pulp almost and despite the efforts of his mother, Kat and his partner, picked him up by the throat and threw him down two flights of stairs.

He didn't know it then, but that release changed him forever as a character. He had always cared for other people's troubles; now he was always ready to commit to actually helping them to the best of his ability. He had always tried to avoid or talk his way out of physical confrontations of a violent nature; now he had no real fear of anyone and was incapable of ever backing down, regardless of the risk to himself, and most telling of all, he had always had final control of his temper and actions. Now, he knew that in certain circumstances he had no control at all.

His widowed mother was incapable of being left on her own. Charlie and Tracey sold their flat, bought the family bungalow East Uckfield from his mother, and he commuted back to Woodward Essex every day. Tracey tried her best, but of course, it was never going to work. And after four months, she pleaded with Charlie to find a home for his mother on her own. After this, his mother did indeed find a little house in Copthorne some six miles away, but she and Tracey never spoke again. As therapy, she wanted to get back to the business and every day would drive to her old home, never coming down the drive even, look at the garden she had lived and worked in for so many hours with her husband, they had finally been able to get married just two months before he died.

She would change to the passenger seat, and she and her son would drive the long journey to where they had worked together for so many years as a team, their mutual dependency grew stronger and his wife Tracey became less and less by the time he got home in the evening having left his mother to go 'home' to her empty house. He would be naturally tired, resentful of the circumstances, worried about making a living for them all. They would eat some fine dinner she had prepared, but their conversation and understanding of each other became even less than it had been before. Slowly, he began slipping back to Kat. They were together for most of the working day; the physical attraction had never lessened for either of them; she was a sympathetic friend to his mother, and her marriage to Daniel was at an all-time low. Her youngest son was by now twelve and she seriously started talking about divorce.

One night, inevitably, she joined Charlie at the local Boat House Hotel and they both willingly committed adulteries. All the old release for both of them was there, he placated his conscious by thinking that since he had been with Kat before he married, it wasn't really adultery at all, but he also knew there could be no going back once they had started, regardless of the hurt and damage to his wife, Kat's husband and her children, they recommenced the old affair in all its excitement, because they both knew that the strength of their feelings would never fail. The waste she had made of her life and the sheer monotony of her marriage made him want more than ever to put things right for her; give her a share of his much better for her life and make her happy.

They would grab every opportunity to be alone together, making love in empty properties, in the office, in her brother's seedy flat, and once in her own home. Neither of them enjoyed that occasion. It cheapened the relationship; for the first time, it made Charlie seriously think about

Daniel as a real human being with feelings just like his own, a husband who he was cheating on. The direct result was a calming down period whilst they both re-assessed what they were actually doing. Charlie knew Kat's children well, he had no experience of actually living with kids, but if he wanted Kat enough, sure they couldn't be that much of a problem. Besides, Kat didn't intend to bring them with her. She would still see them all every day, and look after their needs; they both convinced themselves that they had thought it through thoroughly. Unfortunately, love blinded the recipients to reality, and their thoughts overlooked all the things they didn't want to think about.

One particularly bad night after an equally frustrating day, he confided the truth to his mother on the drive home. She was appalled; she had no idea that anything had ever been going on between the two of them, and she was frightened of the consequences for everyone, including herself. She threatened to pull out of the business or make him sell it to pay her out. She did in fact refuse to continue working and so he did the daily journey alone from then on, staying after work for an extra hour of passion with Kat and arriving home to by now very suspicious wife. She had taken to checking and inspecting his clothes in the way that wives do in such circumstances.

Kat probably deliberately had started to use musk, and even driving along with his shirt tied to the car's ariel failed to eradicate it fully. More often than not, he merely caught colds from wearing a damp shirt and driving stripped to the waist in the winter. One night, he had reached the stage where discovery would be a relief, and although he would admit nothing, he no longer offered any denial, a week of silence between the two unsure until Tracey said that the position now was hopeless and it would be better for both if he left in the morning. That night, as they lay side by side in bed for the last time, they held hands and cried together, but they neither could embrace and it was over; neither of them slept and at first light, Charlie bundled his clothes into a couple of bin liners and drove away.

He moved into his mother's house and since Kat was still afraid to take the plunge, life went on. After some weeks, Tracey asked him to go back and try again, but he was in love with Kat, not just having an affair. There was no way of a reconciliation between Tracey and his mother and he in fact agreed to buy a bigger house for his mother. Kat in the meantime had gone off the country to run her parent's pub, as her father had been stricken with a heart attack, Charlie had visited her there. After a long time, they spent most of the night together, making love in a beautiful Swedish pine chalet by the riverside; he woke alone of course, longing for the time when they would just be able to wake up together.

On the hottest night of the year, they managed this for the first time. Kat had come back to see her children, and presumably even her husband, and by claiming to both him and her parents that she was staying with the other, she and Charlie booked into the Epping Post House, one wrong phone call would have exposed him, but she was past caring and on that first full night together, they had a leisurely meal, and the most successful union either of them could ever have imagined. They weren't counting and their final total ever afterwards varied depending on which was reminiscing. Surprisingly, Kat's figure was higher than

Charlie's, who could never remember anything past ten, certainly, they got their money's worth out of the shower room. In the morning, both being bubbling over with happiness, Charlie for the sheer devilment said in a loud voice within hearing of a group of overnighters, "Thank you very much, my dear, I consider that money very well spent, and I shall be sure to recommend you to all my friends." Kat exited in haste.

Tracey by this time had put in for a divorce on the grounds of irreconcilable breakdown; she still wanted him back, and although it was still possible in theory, in practice, he was still hoping rather that Kat would do something decisive. One night, this changed dramatically. He and Kat were just sitting down to dinner in a local café, she had come up again to see her kids when Charlie's partner came in to say there was an urgent phone call. It was Tracey in a terrible state; she had just arrived home to find she had been burgled. Charlie told her to wait with the neighbours and drove down faster than he had ever driven before; his mind was filled with remorse and guilt, how could he have left her alone so this could happen?

Supposing it had happened when she was in bed, he knew she had been involved in two frantic affairs since the split up. One to the typical sort of friend who hung around wives just waiting to take advantage, neither of them the type to be there for her when she needed it. He knew he still had a kind of love for her. It was impossible for him to just switch her off completely as if she had never existed, but he knew it wasn't enough for her, and after all, his revived love for Kat had given him the strength to make the break. It was going to work, he believed that more than anything else, but still as he sped down the familiar route to this old home, the feeling grew that Tracey really needed him, and his own desires could not be worth the pain it was causing her.

His memory raced with the recollections of their happier days, and he forgot for the moment the bad times and their causes. He was going home to help her; that must mean something he would just have to try and build on it for her sake if not for his own. Kat had not taken her chance, maybe she never would, this must be the catalyst that fate had thrown in to bring them back together almost against themselves. She would be waiting in distress when he got there, he would take her in his arms and the future would take care of itself, it was his karma, as Buddhists believe, and you can't change your karma, can you?

The lights were on, the front door was open, the poor little fool, she must be frightened to death; he raced through the front door, he was home, there waiting for him was …The dragon lady. Icy, hating, malevolent loving each moment of it and in ten seconds, it was all gone.

One of the best and the most satisfying rows of all time raged with no holds barred. It made Katherine Hepburn/Peter O'Toole scenes from 'The Lion in Winter' pale by comparison, the final line from that scene 'What Families Don't Have Their Ups and Downs' had long been one of Charlie's favourite quotes, but this wasn't family; this was the enemy; she of limited vocabulary, never had a verbal chance. Charlie had in full swing had a way with words that he polished to perfection over the years; her invective and her spite were reduced to open-mouthed eye-popping disbelief. He told her alright; boy, did he tell her, and he left what had been his parents and then his own home for the last time ever.

It cost him of course as he knew it would because mummy-in-law took over the settlement claim. Charlie had never really cared what the final figure would be. He wanted to make sure Tracey had enough for a new home of her own plus whatever else he could afford and then a bit more. He owed her that at least, what he didn't know was that as he was a partner in a business of his own, that also was an asset that she could claim half of. It crippled him for years after, because in order to settle the claim, he had to get the firm to pay him half of his total partnership value. He remained a senior partner, if they ever sold up, he would only get the balance.

Chapter 5
Go Back and Start Again

He had just enough left to buy a small rather uninviting converted flat in Woodward, but it was there immediately and it was at best a roof over his head, and there was always Kat; there was his mother too of course. During the divorce, he had taken out a rented flat, where his mother used to stay during the week; she started to do the same in the new one. He was on his own and there were at least company for each other. And then after all this time just after he moved in, Kat left Daniel; she left her home, her youngest son stayed with his father and paternal grandmother; her other children had started work, she was there finally all the mistakes could be forgotten; it was going to work; it had to; it didn't.

Within six months, the magic had gone to be replaced by rows and arguments. Charlie started going back to his mother's home at weekends. Kat stayed at the flat. When his mother did come up to stay overnight during the week, Kat would go out. The couple who had worked so well together in the business failed miserably together as a pair; her children who he had liked immensely before became a constant source of annoyance and anger.

He knew how repeating the very same mistakes as his stepfather, these youngsters as teenagers were impossible. They demanded; they took everything from their mother; she tried all the time to overcompensate to them and Charlie seethed. They were forever getting into trouble with authority; their own father could never be told; he would just get violent with them, all Charlie's tact and reason were to no avail. 'You're not my father. You can't do anything to us.'

A 17-year-old daughter with a foul mouth and no self-control at all, with a penchant for bringing home greasy-haired pimply rockers of the kind to give Charlie apoplexy and climbing all over them kissing and cuddling in front of everyone, one of her favourites actually stole her watch and jewellery and that was the last seen of him. But it made no difference to her; the next was just as bad.

A 15-year-old boy with a lovely disposition, but feeling his oats and always in one scrape of the other, and a sullen 12-year-old with no manners at all and a remarkable talent for being unteachable in anything; yes, they had their good points, but only their mother could see them. The excitement and passion had gone from their sex life; after all, it was possible any time now.

One Saturday morning, Kat told Charlie she was leaving and that weekend, she moved lock, stock and barrel into a rented house with her brother. She found a new job and that was that. Charlie felt little remorse; he actually felt quite relieved, but he hated being lonely. Still, he thought *I am only 37, you can still roll with it when you're young, there will soon be another one along, and I am a bachelor again, even if I am a bit hard up*. He was right, there were others along, but he had forgotten that he wasn't of the type that could easily pull birds. The only really decent ones were those who got to know him first and went for his personality and caring, not his looks or sex appeal. What he got was a quite attractive blonde in her early twenties, who was a telephonist in his friend Aidan's solicitor's office. They got drunk together at the office Christmas party, but she was thick as a plank incapable of any conversation or depth and known at work as daft Alice. Apart from passionate embraces, she refused anything else.

One night when he was out with her, and she was a sloppy drunk, he ran into Kat in an Indian restaurant and was highly embarrassed to be seen thus. Kat was with quite a nice ordinary guy, and Charlie was ashamed of what he was with, so that was the end of daft Alice. Next, via a dinner date with some old friends, he met a recent divorcee; she had two obnoxious small sons and her husband had left her for another younger woman. She did have a very nice townhouse; she was warm and comfortable and ran her own business, but looks-wise, she hadn't got it. She was at least three-stone overweight, and going to bed with her was nothing more than comforting. Fate reared its head again once more in Charlie's life; on the night he had seen Kat again, he had also been with an old drunken friend, known to every pub in the area as fat Ron, then about 50, with a real beer gut and short silver hair, one of the lads in every sense of the word, and great fun to be with.

He had not known that Kat was free, but he very soon did something about it. Kat by then was working for an old associate of Charlie's, in a job he had introduced her to, a singularly unsuccessful estate agent, who had struggled for years to keep going. He had enjoyed a most successful charisma bypass and as a salesman had the unique distinction of hiding behind a screen every time someone came in his office forgetting that his feet could be seen at the bottom and when he wasn't selling a house, which was most of the time he was trying to sell heat machines, small thin bearded and very Jewish. He was a joke figure in the trade.

Kat had him like a whirlwind, revolutionised his organisation, spent money like water, which was her way, and initially made him a visible entity at last. He had made her a junior profit-sharing partner of sorts. Charlie had explained to her that at the end of the day, any sharing would depend on just what the senior partner decided was a profit or not, but she was enjoying her prestige too much to care and she was good. About six weeks after they met, Kat announced that she and Fred were engaged, and about to be married.

Charlie was initially totally disbelieving and found the idea too ridiculous to even contemplate. He hadn't missed her at all and by this time lonely and fed up with his singular lack of progress in meeting anyone worth knowing, he had started to miss his ex-wife even more; he knew she had bought a nice flat in Horley and had got a ground job in Gatwick. He hated the way they had ended, and having jailed in his great love for Kat, he wanted them to be at least friends if possible. No matter what the circumstances at the time, he had remained close friends eventually with every girl he had ever been involved with and over the years they all kept in some sort of touch.

Tracey was the only exception, but then she was the only one he had married. On the day of their divorce, they had talked, really talked probably for the first time and parted sadly, so now he rang her and asked her for a dinner date. She met him for the evening; they had an hour or so of reminiscing and brought each other up to date on what they had been doing and who with. And she told him there was no one regular at that time and was of course delighted to hear that Kat was off the scene. They discussed their various mothers, seeking various solutions 'If we get back together' and it did not seem so impossible after all. The following week, he saw her again; this time with a bunch of flowers and the best of intentions. She invited him into her flat. He was greeted with a hungry kiss, and it was obvious that she expected him to stay the night.

He had given her the entire contents of their old home and as he sat on his settee, looking at his TV and drinking from their Noritaki China wedding present set, he did indeed relax and began to let go of his doubts once again, surely they could sort out the old problems once and for all, then Tracey misread the situation and made a major miscalculation; she began using her bullying tactics of her mother. She felt Charlie had come back with his tail between his legs and that she was in the ascendancy. And as he listened, it became as if the dragon woman herself had been personified before his eyes. She dictated terms that completely excluded any relationship other than distance from his own mother and insisted on pushing her own to the front.

Charlie felt it slipping away before him again; the intervening 18 months had changed nothing, but he said nothing. *Always leave the door slightly open*, was an axiom he lived by, but he knew as he left that he was chasing shadows.

Kat's wedding plans had proceeded apace and were only three weeks away. And although he well thought she might be trying some complicated con, to make him jealous or bringing him back, Charlie was not particularly perturbed, if it was a con, she was wasting her time and if it was true, it was so stupid to do it on so obvious a rebound that she deserved what she got. What they had enjoyed together was just as gone, as it was with Tracey for different reasons.

Once again, fate or coincidence reared its head. He had not had any communication with Kat for weeks and one Friday night when he was out for a drink with one of his oldest friends Callum, they went on impulse to the local country club. They knew the owner well for years, and Friday night was a good time to meet girls there. He did not think Kat would in fact be there this close to her impending nuptials, but Zaira, one of her casual friends who was single might well be and it was worth a try. Neither of them had been to the club for weeks anyway, and so they went; there was no sign of anyone they knew and whilst standing with his back to the bar just watching the dancing, Charlie suddenly felt familiar arms go around him, and a very familiar body pressed against his back; it was she of course, and of all the bars in all the world, she had chosen just this one night to come down for a last time.

They danced closely and indeed she did look lovely. She had a brand-new very topical Afro hairstyle all stickie-out curls, which suited her perfectly and obviously she wanted him to come home with her there and then. Charlie became the macho man immediately intending as he thought to have one more night of passion and walk away in the morning. *That would stop the nonsense with Fred* he thought, *then I'll be the one to play hard to get and we will have a relationship on my terms for a change.* Indeed, he had to admit that she was arousing him, but all the better, he would give her a night to remember all right. He did indeed, one of his very best and most athletic performances ever with her, including his speciality walking round the room whilst in action jobs, which he had originally done his back in back in a bungalow, but what started by him reminding her of his prowess, developed unexpectedly into real lovemaking with tenderness and care for her enjoyment settling back eventually totally sated with each other.

He began to think how much he would enjoy having breakfast with Kat and her flatmates in the morning. They had been particularly noisy, mostly because he knew the other girls were listening and he was thinking of how he would appear to them in the kitchen, modestly but pointedly remarking how tired Kat looked and them thinking lucky girl. Kat then pulled her masterstroke of all time, she looked at her alarm clock and said, "Thank you, darling, that was a lovely, goodbye, but you really must go now before anyone notices you. We have brought the date forward to next Thursday week. I have so much to do. I won't have time to see you again. Don't make too much noise on your way out, will you?"

Charlie was flabbergasted, deflated, his pride mortally injured, and worst of all, had the tables turned on him with a vengeance. It was 5 a.m. and he was literally turned out in the cold; he could not believe it. He spent one of the worst weekends of his life, unable to sleep or eat. And at 6 a.m.,

Monday, he made his decision, finally and irrevocably he had to have her, so he rang her and proposed there and then. For the first time, he was certain, sure of what he wanted for life. She paused for too long and then said firmly, "Right now, the answer is 'no,' but I will think about it and let you know."

Once again, she had caught him cold. He never expected for a moment anything other than acceptance; he had led their relationship for years, how could it now be so reversed? He expected her to call back at any moment, but when after two whole days and nights, she still had failed to contact him, he got really agitated; he would walk around to her flat in the early hours to check if she was in, not to see her but just to check. Sometimes her car was there; more often, it wasn't; then horrors of horrors, one night Fred's car was there as well. By the end of the week, he was a zombie, time was running out fast, what could he do, he could fight of course, he used every ploy in his repertoire he could not, would not give up whilst there was a chance. Finally, late Monday evening, she agreed.

She rang Fred there and then and told him nicely and firmly, that she made a mistake; he knew it had been too quick and although she liked him immensely, he knew she didn't love him enough to make the final commitment. She told him that she now realised Charlie was the only one who really understood her, and that she was going to take the chance with him because she knew him so thoroughly, and all their mutual problems had been ironed out, he was sad but not shattered. He had expected it anyway because he knew all along where her true love lay and indeed, he only expected companionship from a pretty girl, which would he hoped to have been enough for both of them.

There were still two full days before 15 September. All licences had to be altered. The necessary certificates and documents were all found. The next morning, Charlie took champagne around to Kat's office, and they shared it with the window cleaner. She notified her parents who refused outright to acknowledge the wedding; they rang Charlie's mother who promptly collapsed and refused to come. Charlie came down with near-terminal flu but come the morning and there they were waiting at the Barking registry office; Charlie in his brand-new suit with a nose bright red, and his head stuffed with tablets. Kat looked happy and lovely wearing a cream outfit, the best man was her boss, looking more spastic than ever, and Kat's brother who had come at the last moment with his own new bride, who Kat quite rightly hated and Kat's best friend Beatrix, and that was it.

The registry office in Barking was one of the most unappetising buildings in the area; the road itself was a dump. Off they went for lunch in what later became the Bijou French Restaurant in South Woodward. But at that time was called Wedges and was owned by special friends of Charlie's.

He in fact had sold it to them and it was their favourite eating place, word got out somehow and the quiet lunch for six, which was about all Charlie could afford in ready cash, grew to a party of 60-plus; friends and acquaintances came from all directions. They were all laughing at the fact that when it came time to read out the father's names during the service, Charlie snorted uncontrollably on learning Kat's father's middle name was Oliver, to be followed by Kat's giggling when Charlie's father's name was read out as Lucas.

Kat's daughter turned up and then unbelievably Charlie's mum arrived she had been travelling since early morning, had been traipsing round Ilford for hours and had missed the wedding by ten minutes; a lovely party atmosphere developed, a cake was delivered and for the first time that he had ever seen, Charlie's mother got drunk and sentimental. This wedding arranged on the spur of the moment, completely the opposite of his first meticulously planned one, was a winner from the start.

It was only slightly marred when Charlie accepted a phone call from his cousin Sandra, a slim young blonde who had carried an unrequested love for him since childhood, who was ringing him to suggest a date, as she had just heard through the family that he was free again, and who when he told her that she was actually talking to him at his wedding reception, gave a piercing shriek of disbelieve and hung up.

Eventually, when the bar bill had risen to over £500, a month's wages in those days, they called it a day. Staggering back to Kat's flat with fish and chips, the only food they had eaten all day, Charlie spent not only his honeymoon night but the next two days dying of flu. His friend Jack the barman obligingly cut the bar bill down to £50 cash, which went straight to his pocket and life began again for Charlie and Kat.

Chapter 6
Repeat Performance

He was pretty hard up by this time, and it was quite difficult at first for the two of them. The property market was quiet, and since both relied exclusively on house sales for a living and he only had a few thousand pounds left of his savings, there wasn't much left for extras. He had one more obligation to perform for his mother. It was bad enough for her that her new house had to be cancelled and suddenly she was alone again, down in the country, but she had persuaded him to take her away for a once-in-a-lifetime holiday in America. It was all booked and prepaid for although it was the last thing he wanted to do; and the separation from Kat just two weeks after the marriage was unimaginable.

He felt he owned her that much at least and both he and Kat knew that if they ever expected to heal from the break with his mother, this would be the best way to do it. Before the new life overtook him, he had been quite excited by the prospect of going again to the States. And he had carefully arranged just the sort of tour that his mother's age would be able to stand. It was an expensive one, of course, but to his mother, it was the achievement of a lifetime's ambition, Arthur would never have taken her and thus this was her one and only chance, reluctantly, but putting on the best face he could, Charlie tore himself away from Kat and off they went.

It started with a bang, all right. Their seats were occupied by an Arab family, who professed no knowledge of English and could not be moved. The only two other vacant seats on the whole Jumbo were widely separated and Charlie, of course, had an intimate knowledge of airline procedure, promptly took position by the first-class lounge and refused to accept anything other than the seats that they had bought and paid for. The result was just as anticipated and they were duly ushered into the first-class section, only about a quarter full. Another of those coincidences occurred that seemed to rule his life in so many ways. They could have been placed anywhere but where they were seated, they were just two places away from the nearest other passengers.

At first glance, this other passenger was of little interest, a tall tanned man with thinning hair, wearing a scruffy tracksuit and Gucci sneakers. His eyes were hidden by dark glasses and then recognition dawned; of all the famous actors whose films Charlie had enjoyed over and over again, those of Gary Cooper, the early John Wayne and Burt Lancaster were his favourites of all time, with Clint Eastwood and Sean Connery. They were between them; the one who had made all his favourite movies, and there large as life was Burt himself.

Charlie knew every film he had ever made since his days as a Beefcake acrobat to his emergence as one of the finest all-round actors. As people came up to him and introduced themselves to him, he would switch on his trademark—dazzling smile for about ten seconds. After about an hour, they got into conversation. Charlie had a deep interest in military history, his knowledge of the Zulu was encyclopaedic; he had always been fascinated by the tragedy and mistakes that led to the biggest single disaster British troops had ever suffered. Zulu was his favourite film, and he knew every word of the dialogue. He had been waiting for ages for the sequel to be made, he had met Sean Connery and Stanley Baker at a golf tournament in Copthorne years before; they had told him then that another was being planned and here was Burt, just returning from the last location shooting in South Africa of Zulu Dawn.

Charlie was certainly the only person on the whole plane who had any conception of what it was about. And the long flight passed in a flash, leaving him with a memory to cherish. The holiday itself was interesting; his mother had the time of her life but he missed Kat dreadfully even though, he realised that had she been with him, she would have loved things they saw together, but the deep need to understand then like he did, would not have materialised, there just was no one, who could be close enough mentally to know what was inside his very soul. And share with him on that level, how could there ever be, it was impossible.

He walked again to the harbour in San Francisco, the Grand Canyon, and Las Vegas. He went to Washington for the first time and Niagara Falls; he fell in love with New York, a city that had left him cold before, he enjoyed his mother's pleasure, but again really, he was alone. A chance remark in Washington amazed him; a young woman on an adjoining table overheard his conversation and turned out to be an ex-client whose house he had sold years before. She was there for that one night only, neither of them had recognised each other, but Charlie had been explaining yet another coincidence from his past when arriving at the San Francisco bus depot with Tracey, they had found the hotels all full, and Tracey had gone off in a cab to the poorer part of town to see what she could find.

She registered in an area they had no intention of ever going to, came back for him and as the two of them checked in at the reception desk, the day manager came off duty looked up in amazement and said, "Hello, Charlie, do you want your usual?" He was the ex-barman at the Red Lion in Woodward Green, and this was his last day of working there. When this girl in Washington heard Charlie mention the name of the pub, the coincidence compounded itself yet again. And that was the story of Charlie's life.

Charlie and Kat moved into a rented Queen Anne townhouse, luxuriously remodelled and fully furnished, 100 yards from the Red Lion. They had their own ensuite bathroom for the first time, and the main bathroom had a huge double three-corner bath, which they enjoyed to the full, their social life was full and happy and for the first two years; they were completely content with each other. Charlie had been invited to join the local Rotary club, a very elite and special club indeed, having had Sir Winston Churchill no less as a member. He would sit and look at the past presidents' honours board, marvelling at the well-known local names on it dating back to the thirties and he came to be totally involved with doing local community work and being accepted as a team member by all these older and more successful local businessmen.

He remembered cringing with embarrassment the first time he was expected to stand up and talk to them. He was fine in his own right amongst his friends; what he lacked in physical looks and tried to compensate for with an incisive and clever sense of humour, usually self-mocking, but with an immediate natural and polished edge; he was fine in his own environment with his clients on a one to one basis; he had total confidence in himself at that level, and could more than hold his own in any company, but to stand up and be counted in front of an audience, that was a different ball game; he faked laryngitis and anything else he could think of, to put off the awful day when he would have to explore his lack of experience and when eventually, he forced himself to take the floor, the kindest thing to be said about it was that it was brief. He could seldom remember having felt so inadequate and embarrassed, but it had been a fear inside him for years.

He had been made to face it and once he had conquered it, the obvious transformation occurred and as his confidence in himself grew, he became one of the most vocal members of the club. On his feet at the drop of a hat, he started studying other speakers, politicians, and actors. He borrowed a bit here and an inflexion there and within a year, at just over forty, he had reached the stage where on a good day, he really could achieve attention, hold the interest of an audience of any size, and always amuse them. This, of course, opened new horizons for him. He had never wanted to organise or administrate anything, he left things to the last moment and then got the task done as quickly as possible, that was his way his whole adult life, but for him, it worked.

He took over the reputation originally applied to a friend of his, who was claimed to be a late starter, who once he began then moved with precision and decision. He liked that and people did in fact think that was the way he was; he wasn't, of course, and things he organised on his own usually ended in a last-minute muddle, but again, they did all work, and he achieved some quite remarkable results. He organised a huge fund-raising event single-handed, others in the club tried it before, but his was the biggest of the lot. And the net funds raised provided enough for a complete minibus.

He organised race nights, having to do the commentary himself one night when the sound system broke down. Kat got used to attending various functions with him, no way was she going to be left out if she could help it, and she was invited to join the wife's own parallel club. Now this struck Charlie as really funny, the other wives were mostly matronly; big hats and big bosoms, mostly reflecting in their husband's local prominence, and nearly without exception, the worst type of provincial tory snobs. Kat with her veneer of assumed respectability was just under the surface some lovely east-end born and bred girl that Charlie had found irresistible; her misuse of words she had picked up from him, her excitable way of speaking when words had to just burst out of her regardless, and visually noisily was a source of kindly amusement to him. It annoyed the hell out of her own family, who thought she was assuming airs and graces. And that too caused amusement to Charlie. So, by all means, he told her, but you will hate it.

Privately, he thought she would be like a fish out of water, again he had misjudged her, she loved it and the other women took to her on her own level. Thus, the two of them entered their prestige stage. Charlie found a quiet pleasure in being recognised and acknowledged, but equally, he had come to appreciate the help that less fortunate members of society needed. To him, that was what Rotary was all about. And he felt better about himself as a person, to be put back in time and care, rather than just take out of the community all the time as before, he had developed a conscience at last, other people's needs genuinely concerned him and it showed. Together he and Kat revelled in their newfound social success, and it kept them interested in what each other was doing. Sadly, the same was not true of their real life together.

Time had eroded their passion; it was still good, but it was better for her than for him. That wouldn't have mattered in the long run, their friends next door, politely suggested they close the bedroom windows at night so that they could get some sleep. So the pair of them was still more than active, but outside interference had begun to take its toll. Daphne, Kat's daughter, became a frequent visitor, but at 19, she was more impossible than ever. Blackmailing her mother's guilt complex, taking all and giving nothing; Charlie never interfered, but inwardly, he seethed one Christmas when Kat had gathered all three children together and made every effort to please them.

Daphne, having spent the whole afternoon in a drunken sleep, announced that she was off to a party; her mother was deeply hurt and dared to suggest that this one special day she had hoped they could all be together as a family. Her daughter immediately flew into a rage, screaming and swearing and Kat slapped her face; losing all control, Daphne went for her mother physically. She was a big girl, taking after her father and Charlie was forced to take action. He manhandled her down the stairs and kicked her backside through the garden door. He told her that since she was such a pain in the ass to everyone else, she might as well have a real one. But Christmas, of course, was ruined.

Alexander, the 13-year-old, was resentful, rude and feeling his adolescent feet, and he also had an uncontrollable temper. He was small for his age but very cocky, he manipulated his mother's emotions and was a constant cause of hurt to her. Charlie tried explaining to him, reasoning with him and helping him. It was like talking to a brick wall and inevitably, he ran out of patience as the years went by. He tried and tried to reach both Daphne and Alexander, but they were jealous of his taking their father's place with their mother and Charlie just did not have the knowledge to cope with them. They came from a background and lifestyle that he had never known himself; he had his own experience of his childhood with a stepfather of course, but sympathy was not enough for these two. It didn't cause any rows between him and Kat, but her distress hurt him, and his patience was exhausted with them.

One bright spot was the middle child Kirill; he had his mother's disposition, a lovely sense of humour and an innate kindness that was irresistible. Everyone liked Kirill, big and bumbling, he was like an amiable bear. If it could break, Kirill broke it, whatever he touched, and being inquisitive, he touched everything and it came apart in his hands. He was lovely, but he was also harebrained, and the troubles he got into were endless. Charlie never did lose patience with him, but as he ambled from disaster to disaster, he did get fed up to the back teeth with having to pay for repair bills. He had a very bad motorcycle accident, breaking his leg; the boy moved in with them and totally overwhelmed the home for months.

To save Kat's squeamishness, Charlie was the one who had to clean the boy's leg; a steel bolt had been drilled through the bone, which needed taking out every night and the hole became infected, sniffing up close for traces of gangrene which Kirill was sure he had contracted, was not exactly Charlie's idea of fun, but it had to be done, and it was too upsetting for Kat on her own, so he coped. Kirill was his success at that time, one out of three was the best he could achieve, and with the other two, it was an armed truce.

Chapter 7
All Together Now

Kat in the meantime lost her partnership, predictably there was no monetary value to it and Charlie was glad to see the end of it. He could foresee that the spastic tycoon could easily run huge Bills, which as his partner, Kat would be partly responsible for; this meant he would be. He had taken Kirill's' accident claim to his friend Aidan's Solicitors Practice, to be sorted out and became very involved in trying to present it in its best light, not easy as the boy had been very drunk, had been doing wheelies and hadn't paid his licence or insurance. Aidan managed to get him £2000 compensation, which said a great deal about his skills. Kirill blew the lot in six weeks flat and gradually, all these things mounted up in Charlie's disappointment.

Kat had decided that she still wanted her own business. Charlie's mother wanted to back her and work with her and it was agreed. What the area needed was the sort of coffee house which ladies out shopping could use, morning snacks, light lunches and afternoon teas, not just the KFC bar type, something 'nice.' A working men's snack bar came on the market and having worked out all the figures, Charlie said, " Ok, but not if it means working yourselves to death."

The result was the Shrubberies Coffee house in South Woodward, 50 yards from Sainsbury's, it could hardly fail. He warned Kat one last time, this was the last of his capital was she sure she knew what she was letting herself into, to be careful, and not spend anything unless the money was there to pay for it. She was adamant it would make her happy; she knew what she was doing after all she and Daniel had owned a pub of their own; this trade was far easier. So, Toni's Diner, scruffy, cheap and nasty, but highly profitable, was transformed into a pleasant, smart, highly non-profitable, disaster.

Poor Kat caught salmonella just before opening time, so it sat there empty for weeks. When it did finally start, it was popular enough, but how many coffees and teas do you need to sell to make a profit? Charlie's mum tried her hand at being a waitress, which lasted two days, Charlie would rush up the road from his estate agency at lunchtime, transform himself into a waiter for the peak hour, rush back to work until 6.30, go back to the café until 8, clear up, wash, clean up and count up the takings. The last task of course was the one that took the least time. No one minded working that hard to build up a new business, but this one was just losing money, not making it.

The decision was made to open in the evenings for full meals as a bistro; this meant hiring a chef. And Charlie was impressed most by a young chap who came all the way down from Darlington, just for an interview. He turned out to be a good enough cook, but chef he wasn't. He was a good enough thief as well, and he was lazy. Because he was homeless, Charlie got him a rented flat, putting up the initial deposit and advance rent. And when he was finally sacked on the spot, the rent arrears and debts that they had stood guarantors for all had to be honoured. Then Kat had to have an urgent operation on the nerves in her wrists, one at a time, which needed her to be off for six weeks; the only available person to run the place, turned out to be an alcoholic, and the business ran down to nothing.

Kat was determined to save it and as soon as she was well enough, The Shrubberies Coffee house/bistro/restaurant reverted into being Kat's café. She would go there at 6.30 every morning to do workmen's breakfasts and work through to 8 p.m. every night, six days a week, whilst Charlie tried to sell and cut their losses.

Eventually, the nightmare ended and they managed to clear enough to pay all their debts, but his mother had lost £8000, and it hurt their relationship deeply. Starting again in a small modern flat that he could just about afford, Charlie managed to recoup some capital on some property deals; they travelled to Italy, where he loved showing her Rome, the Leaning Tower of Pisa, Sorrento and Capri and they walked up Mount Vesuvius, lighting their cigarettes in the bowl of the volcano, viewing the explicit, erotic paintings and statues at Pompeii with the three-legged centurion. They had enjoyed their first holiday together on the Isle of Elba, walking for hours in the mountains and tracing the footsteps of Napoleon; this second trip seemed to calm things down between them.

Later, they took Charlie's mum to Rhodes, and this helped to bring the three of them back together again. The children were of course teenagers now, except for Daphne who was coming up to 21. She seemed to have calmed down a bit and did in fact at this time enter the police force as a cadet, but she was still very difficult to cope with.

And then in the ordinary course of business, Charlie came across a unique property, the likes of which as an ordinary suburban estate agent he had never been instructed on before. It was a very large Victorian house, which for years had been used as a world-famous boarding school for deaf children, in a main road position, full of character and interest, but in a most uninviting residential situation. To him, it was like an oasis in a sea of mediocrity. It pulled him inexorably; he spent two hours there the first time he viewed it, and he was at a loss as to how to value it; he knew immediately that he was going to have to buy it somehow, his moral dilemma was that the owners trusted him to price it fairly, which would put it beyond his reach and in the end, he compromised and gave them two figures, one as an optimistic asking price, which he would try for and a lower one which he advised them they might have to think about later, and which in was in fact the price he could afford himself.

He then marketed the property for them, but he didn't exactly pull out all the stops, and the months went by; eventually, he went back to the owners and they agreed to sell it to him as the original lower figure. There had been some interest from other would-be buyers which was a chance he felt he had to take after all; at the very least, there was a nice fat commission to be earned. He dragged negotiations through for another six months, and then at the age of 42, he, Kat and his mother took the biggest and the last chance of all.

Chapter 8
Risky Business

They knew it was a bargain, but it could easily turn into a white elephant well, and having actually bought it, what the hell were they going to use it for? A nursing home would have produced the best income, but none of them were trained for that, and Charlie hated the idea of making money from old people, no matter what the income. They really had scrapped the barrel in getting it in the first place and had enough left to convert it into whatever they finally decided. The local council would give them a grant to make it into a DHSS hostel or for student accommodation, but they decided that the best use for them would be to turn it into a hotel.

Before any work actually started, just a few weeks after they moved in, Daphne prevailed up her mother to let her hold her 21st birthday party there, much against Charlie's better judgement; well over 200 fancy-dressed drunks invaded the place. The entire class of cadets came, most of the male cadets dressed as Hitler or other Nazis, which went down like a real balloon with some Israelis someone else invited. Kirill and his friends came as Rastafarians, with amazing make-up, which also went down like a lead balloon with the cadets, who were so drunk that they thought the rustas were real, and therefore fair game for abuse and police brutality, they did teach them well at Hendon.

The whole affair degenerated into a mass orgy working the swinging sixties at its most permissive, drugs and booze were everywhere, and there was mass copulation in every conceivable place, conceiving in fact seemed to be the most popular idea of the night. They were coupled in the bath, on the landings, in Charlie's car in the garage, in the boiler room, in the greenhouse and in the garden shed. What was going on in the bedrooms themselves was at least hidden from view, but from the movement and noises emanated from behind the closed doors, it was just as well that the Victorians built houses to last.

Apart from being jealous as hell, Charlie was, to say the least, dismayed by the carnage, but it was Kat's daughter, it was her 21st and once again, he shrugged it off; after all, it had been one hell of a party. The last time he had experienced anything like that was in his own early twenties, when he had met and gone to bed with two school teachers, one of the most formative experiences of his early life, and a memory that often returned to him with pleasure and some puzzlement, with so many orifices available, he could never remember who was doing what and to whom or even how he had managed, but that also had been one hell of a party, so how could he criticise this one.

Slowly, the hotel came together, first as a guest house and then after a further year of fighting the council and an appeal that he spent months preparing, everything came right at last. They were in business; it was working between three of them and they were making very good money at last.

Chapter 9
Prestige Time

Charlie had at the same time been doing very well in his Rotary work; it had become a large part of his life, in between the two businesses, he had found time to involve himself deeply in voluntary work, he started working at Crisis for Christmas every Christmas Eve, collecting clothes and blankets all day, driving a bread van full of the day's unsold cakes and bread up to east end, serving food for the night's meal.

On his first attempt, he ended up scrubbing down and hosing off the derelict end of the affluent society, genuine down and outer who were given a Christmas in the warm, cleaned up and fed and reclothed, the fact they immediately sold their clothes for booze money was irrelevant, Charlie knew he had tried and that was enough. Kat's closest friend was Beatrix, they had known each other for years, and her daughter Danya who was also 21 started going on these working trips with him. She was beautiful and intelligent, but fated to be unhappy in love; her mother had been married three times and had a whole string of failed affairs. Danya having been brought up in a single-parent home, where there was no regular father figure, was rootless herself and in many ways, she looked on Charlie as a substitute figure, sharing her secrets and hopes with him. They became lasting friends, and when she had troubles, she couldn't manage, she would turn to him first for help; she was indeed a very sexy young lady.

Kat recognised the danger signals of course, but Charlie resented her for her suspicions. He became involved in a programme for encouraging youngsters from all walks of life to develop into public speakers; he loved this work, he would actually see these kids start in their first year as nervous inept, stumbling novices and change within three or four years into competent, confident young speakers. His favourites came from the 'better schools,' but from West Ham Boys Club and Shoreditch Air Training Corps, where because of their uniforms he often confused the girls with the boys, he ended up organising and running almost single-handed the competition for the whole of East London, he knew that none of the other areas managed to get more than token teams together.

'His' area grew and grew, and his teams won all the London Finals year after year, an unexpected bonus to this was the election at the age of 44 to the presidency of his own Rotary club; he was very proud of this honour, the first in his life really. His name was up there on the board forever, in the most illustrious company and on merit only, was unheard of for anyone to be elected for at least ten years, and he was the youngest ever. Kat shared this with him, they had travelled with the international Rotary set to Paris, Berlin and Florence and lived for a few days as jet setters each year. Very expensive of course, but of a quality and style that was unbelievable. And here he was on an unadulterated ego trip for a whole year; they could afford it. If they wanted anything extra, he would do one of his property deals.

Kat equally enjoyed her own success in the ladies' organisation, which was mostly a crabby old bunch, but they made her their own Lady President. And this meant she also had to make speeches and attend functions of her own, so Charlie coached her, gave her confidence and wrote most of her addresses for her; some of his very best speeches came during his period. It amazed him that he got the audience's response that he did, most after-dinner speakers were pompous and boring, also he did the reverse most of them laboured to get their point across or bludgeoned the audience into the ground and told the most appalling jokes. Charlie knew better than to tell jokes in public like that, most of his were of the rude variety anyway, so quite simply he was himself, his one-liners were always against himself, it seemed that the whole world was smiling at them and they could do no wrong, the last gamble had paid off. They had made it, life was good.

His own ladies' night was a grand affair, he called it that because it cost him £1000, his family's closest friends, his Rotary and business colleagues, the mayor, who was a personal friend and the local press, all were there. And Charlie was in his very best form; he had spent nearly a month preparing an impromptu speech, but by the time it was his turn, the usual happened and most of what he was going to say had been used so he threw it away and really did make one off his cuff, they loved it.

The presidential party travelled to Germany that year, to a lovely unspoilt seaside resort on the Baltic, feted like minor royalty, Charlie and Kat were the centre of attraction, he was invited by one of the German industrialists to a private meeting on his yacht, they had schnapps to welcome him aboard, more to toast to the anchor coming up, more to celebrate casting off, and by the time they had to drink to the health of the harbour master as they passed him Charlie was past caring where they were going.

Eventually, they stopped for lunch, pumpernickel and salamis, washed down with Irish whiskey, a squall blew up and things got pretty uncomfortable so the rum was passed around, he was handed a fishing rod of great complexity, which even sober he couldn't have managed, and sat with his legs hanging over the side, to tell the truth, boats had never been an attraction to him, he couldn't swim for a start, and then he asked what they were expecting to catch. And was told 'sharks,' he promptly retired to the cabin roof, with memories of jaws sobering him up rapidly. On a different occasion, he was invited to Berlin to attend a big function, his friend the chief of police took him to some of the most notorious clubs in the city, where dancing with a stripper who had just seen him squat on a large full bottle of hock, and who was still carrying it inside her, was to say the least a novelty, and what some girls could do with a live python was amazing, the ladies of the night were certainly arousing, but he kept them at arm's length, well not exactly arms, but enough was enough.

His grand moment came at the main dinner, he was given his own interpreter, who turned out to be the Austrian Ambassador and who mostly translated by saying 'Oh, has not said much of importance' when asked. His old bank manager friend Jeremy had come with him for company and really helped by going around telling everyone that Charlie would not only address them in Germany, but in an accent of Berlin and that he was the best Rotary speaker in London, with this build-up, Charlie approached the speakers' dais, festooned with half a dozen microphones, and with a battery of spotlights nearly blinding him, he pulled out his bilingual speech, only to find Jeremy had switched it for a folded menu, 'Mein Gott.'

Taking a very deep breath, he launched into literally whatever came into his mind first; he could never remember exactly what he did say, he couldn't see them very well, but he could sense that they certainly were not apathetic, so he wound up to the best finish he could think of and offered long live the Rotary club of Berlin, long live the people of Berlin and most of all long live the free and democratic city of West Berlin, clicked his heels and bowed and walked off to an absolute bedlam. They were actually standing on their chairs applauding; never in his days had he felt so self-satisfied, never had he felt such triumph. He pushed his way through the embarrassing throng of back slappers and hand pumpers, these were Germans; they never showed emotion. He sat down, outwardly calm, turned to Jeremy, as if to say 'well' and Jeremy summed it up with one dry sentence, "What happened to the kitchen sink?" He said, which just about summed it up nicely.

Later, his friend Kenneth took him out on yet another boat; this time on the Wannsee Lake, where the border between East and West Berlin runs through the actual water. Now in all the years, he had known the Germans, none of them had ever mentioned 'the war.' They would refer to it obliquely as the period between 1939 and 1945, and they would never be drawn into anything other than vague references as to what they did during this period, some of them by age alone, would have to have been in the services, but they never ever mentioned the Nazis.

Kenneth, who Charlie had met every year and who had become his favourite German, was zooming around the lake when he started pointing out the same sights as the tour guide on an earlier trip, but with an entirely different commentary: Look, there are remains of Hitler's bunker, here is where the brown shirts were massacred in 1936, and then as a piece of de la resistance, you see that island that is where the SS officers trained, you know the SS of course, the ones who murdered the six million Jews, follow that thought Charlie, looking at Waldermar in a new light, whatever happened to Teutonic reticence.

Chapter 10
Clutching at Straws

His year of office finally ended, and in the automatic letdown that followed, he and Kat both seemed to realise that it was the build-up to the whole thing, that had bolstered them in their relationship to each other. Kat and his mother had started arguing together again; he was the man in the middle, and he was fed up to the teeth with never having peace and quiet at home for long. They were all treading on eggshells, business in the estate agency field was going through one of its periodic bad spells, and worst of all was his partner Anton, who Charlie had taken in when his own company collapsed.

Anton had been the only one in fact who had not gone to prison at that time, Charlie had taught him the business from scratch, had later given him a partnership, and had been one of Charlie's closest friends for years. He started to do private deals for himself without any pretence at all. He blatantly said that he was out for number one, do your worst, so Charlie did just that, he sold the company lock stock and barrel to his friend Aidan, who wanted to start the first solicitors and estate agents in the area. Charlie's mother got the bulk of the money, as she should, Charlie got his share less the half he had drawn earlier; Anton got bugger-all. He was very physical and very strong; his favourite trick was to pick up a large full night storage heater every time something dropped down behind it, and another was to hold a car up so that the wheel could be changed without using a jack.

And when he threatened Charlie with actual violence early in their dispute, it really was balls to the walls. Charlie had been very scared at the time, but he had stood and faced him down, not caring what the consequences were. With no peace at all, neither in the home nor in the office, Charlie was seriously tempted by another woman. Relations with Kat had reached the ridiculous stage of her sleeping in a camp bed at the foot of their own; there was very little communication between any of them. She was insanely jealous every time he was out late, accusing him of being with other women and not loving her anymore. He did still love her, but not in the clinging way she required, their love life had become strictly routine and his performance had declined through lack of interest, to the stage that he began to seriously consider he had in fact lost it completely.

They had been more or less constantly active for the best part of 13 years. He was not the sort of man that girls went for on sight, he had never been, but every now and then one would come along unexpectedly, or he would develop a friendship that was fine until he pulled back. He genuinely believed that if it was ok for men to have extramarital affairs; it had to be ok for his partner to do the same, as long as the whole wasn't threatened and neither partner found out. What harm was there really, just don't let it get out of control, he knew Kat wouldn't actually do it herself, but if she had, she might have been less demanding, and he certainly wouldn't have blamed her.

At the start of their marriage, a lovely young Cypriot girl who he knew from Kain, behind the bar part-time in Wedges, took him totally unawares. He had talked with her maybe half a dozen times, and he had no designs upon her at all, never chatting her up, just passing the time of the day. Kat and he had been married on 31 August, a date he could never remember much to Kat's pain. And one snowy night in late October, this girl Clare rang his office to make an appointment to see over an empty house; she was typically Mediterranean in looks and style, had a sensuous figure, and was about 24. They hadn't been in the car for five minutes when out of the blue, she asked him to pull up so they could talk; she said that didn't he realise she was not really interested in seeing the house at all. Didn't he know what it was she wanted?

He was almost at a loss for words; she really was very attractive indeed, but he explained as best as he could, that he was only just married, and had no intention of getting involved, no matter how much he might like to. She told him her family was setting her up in a wine bar of her own, would he be interested in a free partnership? This was from someone he hardly knew. Was she mad? Was it a wind-up? "No," she said; she just knew deep down inside that she could trust him. It was because he had never tried to give her a pull, that made him different to all the other men she met. She wanted someone steady and experienced in her life, and she wanted him right there and then; could they go somewhere, please?

Again, Charlie reminded her that he was a newlywed. She said she hadn't known that, but did it really make any difference, surely, he wasn't one of those boring farts that don't want a bit on the side then. Anything, anything at all would be better than nothing. Charlie walked away from it bemused; things like that just did not happen to guys like him. Clare tried again for several weeks, and on New Year's Eve, when he was in Wedges with Kat. She tried to physically drag him out to the car park that was the lot, afterwards, he tried to avoid her like the plague, and soon left the job, and opened a new place. Kat was safe and never knew, but then she had never been in any danger anyway.

On one other occasion, four or five years later, he met an old girlfriend called Greta, they started drinking wine in the mid-afternoon and by late evening were both very drunk indeed. He remembered that she had been very passionate in the old days, with a truly spectacular figure and on a couple of nights they had spent together, she had taught that jam was not necessarily used exclusively for toast, when you have breakfast in bed and there were places from which to eat a fried egg.

He recently sold her a flat and she took him home to see it. Kat was away somewhere that night and they had been fighting again. What the hell! This was Greta; she was still great looking, her frontal protrusions were still magnificent her face was showing the traces of too much drink over the years, but it was still pretty attractive, they went to bed, but for whatever reason, conscience, guilt, too much drink, nothing really happened he thought about her for a couple of weeks, but he let it go. Kat eventually got into bad physical shape; she was frightened that she would start having fits, and she left home to go and stay with her friend Beatrix in Switzerland.

Charlie took this opportunity to look up Clare again; she was still free had a good business, and her own jaguar, she had hardly aged; she must have been in her late twenties by now. She bought him a meal which was a nice touch, and she took him back to her flat, she was also a very well-developed lady, and as she got undressed and got into bed, she was a real eyeful, but she had a bad migraine and Charlie merely soothed her until she was asleep, thinking about it long and hard and quietly left.

The weeks went by with Kat ringing and writing, telling him she wanted him to come and bring her back; eventually, he decided to do so, and to his great pleasure Beatrix's daughter Danya asked if she could travel with him. They had an unforgettable journey together, first on the ferry, and then on a sleeping car, laughing and playing nearly all night, nothing really occurred, neither of them wanted to spoil their long-time friendly relationship, it was enough that they both knew they could have done. There was one moment of hilarious panic when the train stopped at what Charlie took to be Zurich station; he knew Kat would be waiting on the platform, and frantically started climbing down the ladder from his top bunk.

Before realising that the lower unclothed portion of his anatomy was descending in full view of the commuters waiting patiently on the platform of some suburban station. They had a lovely early breakfast watching the toy town scenery and the mountains, and then they were there, he and Kat had some very serious discussions, enjoyed themselves together for a couple of days, and he told her so that she would understand completely that this was the last break for them. If there ever was another, for whatever reason, for him, there would be no going back on it. It was 'make or break' time for them now, one last very last chance. They both tried. Kat could not change; she was permanently suspicious, and she had accused him 999 times it seemed before the 1000 in time, when she would actually be right.

Chapter 11
The Final Fling

Bella was someone he knew casually; she had a cockatiel the same as Charlie's own Gino; she loved dogs, which she took care of for the RSPSA when they had been injured or neglected and she lived in Fairfield's Road. She had the reputation of being easy and at 34, tall and slender, she was not the sort of woman men could ignore. Charlie was out collecting books door to door; these he would then have shipped out to an orphanage in Africa. He called at her house, knowing it was hers; he had been there before when she was living with her third husband. She had explained then that the two of them had an open marriage, Charlie had no intention of pushing, but equally by now, he knew this time, he would not hold back.

They talked and found that they had a lot in common interest. He thanked her for the books she gave him, asked her if she would care for lunch and changed that to a dinner date on a night that Kat was away somewhere. They did go out together and had a very nice evening. He stayed for coffee still not making any obvious moves; he was pretty nervous about the whole thing, but when she kissed and invited him to stay, he was hooked. There were no excuses;

he wanted her there and then. She aroused him immediately; his only real fear was how he was going to be when it got down to it. It had been years since he had been with another woman; this one was obviously very experienced; could he cope? She was truly amazing, taking him to areas he had forgotten existed, not only did he cope, he excelled himself, his equipment which always looked pretty impressive, lived up fully to his most optimistic hopes.

He remembered a girl once saying to him, "You can do anything you like to with it, except hit me with it." Bella obviously felt the same way. He had thought about Kat earlier and wondered if he would in fact go through with it if it were offered; now he knew, he was glad he had waited this long, the wait for something special had been worth it. In the breaks between, she told him something of her own life; she had been right down on the bottom emotionally and financially and had spent years going from one brief affair to the next; the early ones after her first marriage failed, had been exciting and satisfying for a while. She felt she had turned the clock back to her younger free days again, and for a short time, she had enjoyed that feeling, but the struggle to keep home going on her own, without a regular partner, caused her to get into financial trouble, and she would have lost everything without her family support.

She chose the next man in her life to get married to again, and although she was sure of him before he turned out to be a sadistic bully of the worst kind, she lost her home over him. It was repossessed and after that, she could not trust herself with any men for several years and led the life of a spinster, drinking alone at home, not for pleasure, but to drown her bodily frustrations and loneliness.

Eventually, she met her third husband through her veterinary work. He was quiet, rather nice and very ordinary, just what she thought she needed most. Her family accepted him with relief, but she was too much for him sexually. He had a little previous experience, and instead of being a comfort and support to her, which was what she needed most, he crumbled at the first pressures. He would agree to anything she wanted, but she found having to adopt the leadership in everything meant she might just as well be on her own. He was never on her intellectual or intelligence level and he was boring as well so she bought a very powerful motorbike and suit of skin-tight yellow leathers and started to live her own life once again at 30.

The only job she could get was a social worker, dealing with child abuse, drug cases, single-parent families, etc. The job was too much for her emotionally because of all the distress and at one stage, she ended up as a mortuary attendant. She fought her way back on her own again now and had just been accepted for a new career in the local crown court. Because of the sheer number of affairs she had been involved with, men mostly tended to treat her as cheap and only wanted her for one thing. She had become known as an 'easy lay,' and some of her ex-lovers passed her name and phone number on to their friends. Consequently, it was not unknown for complete strangers to turn up at her home after closing time expecting her to come across in gratitude. Her life had become one long mess.

This touched Charlie sentimentally; he started to think of ways he could maybe help her, but he was uneasy that she had taken him on the first night and decided that lovely it had been, he had better not get himself further involved. The next day, she rang him at work, she told him, she shouldn't phone, that it should have been left up to him, but she was 'climbing the walls'. She said that he was so different from other men she knew; no one had been gentle or caring with her in years and that he had been so good and that even if there was no possible future in it, couldn't she just enjoy him for as long as it lasted?

It lasted just two months, but for that time Charlie was in a different world, all the excitement was there every time she would meet him at the front door dressed in the flimsiest nighties or the high boots. On one occasion, when they went out for a drink, she showed him as they got back in the car that she was wearing only her raincoat and boots. She turned him on left, right and centre. And she would come to his office on a Saturday morning, sitting naked under his desk, whilst he tried to talk to clients in front of him, obviously somewhat handicapped, as he could hardly get up to give them any details of properties; the oral sex she lavished on him drove him mad of such things men weave dreams and fantasies and to Charlie's great relief, his sex drive had returned with a vengeance. He was fatally attracted to her, but he didn't love her, or even pretended to, and consequently, it couldn't last long for either of them.

He was careful not to let Kat find out; he would hide his car in Grove Hill in the car park at the rear of his old flat, or outside the Grove Hotel so that if she followed him, she would look there and find she was imagining things. He did not enjoy this side of the affair, lying to Kat did not come easy. He gave up many opportunities to be with Bella, rather than cheat on Kat, but of course, he knew full well that he was cheating on her every time.

He found her to be a fascinating girl to be with; her intelligence was at least at par with his own, in some respects she was his superior; sexually, he matched her time after time and they revelled in their sensuality. Then one Saturday when they were at the peak of their mutual attraction, Kat walked into the office, she had been waiting outside for the entire lunch hour, whilst she didn't actually catch them or see them in action, it was obvious that she knew, there was of course a bad scene, and Charlie would admit nothing. He dredged up from somewhere a logical explanation, and stuck to it, turning Kat's accusations back against her.

He knew as he was doing this, that it was not a self-defence, he did not want to lose Kat; it was as simple as that. He did not want to hurt her by confirming her worst fears, and he cared enough about Bella not to want her to be dragged into his troubles; she had enough of her own. Kat did not leave that night, and he knew that if she hadn't gone then, she probably wouldn't; he was guilty as hell of course and it had been a horrible shock.

Chapter 12
End of Era

They made up by going for a holiday with some close friends to West Africa; Roots country they saw what purported to be Kunta Kinte village. They played a lot of cards and backgammon together. Charlie won quite a bit of money, but since he had the only backgammon board in the place, he soon lost it round the pool. He found that sitting facing a pair of naked boobs threw his game completely and he lost back to the wives most of what he had won off their husbands. Charlie enjoyed playing with the native children, as much as anything else, they were a real delight and many hours passed happily teaching them and playing with them. He often had a retinue of at least a dozen trailing him and he loved it.

Each village had a head boy, whose job was to chase the other children away from the tourists. Charlie paid one such stick boy to go and chase Kat, telling him that she was only his second wife and that she was being a nuisance the boy did just that with hilarious results. They were shown around the local war cemetery by chance one afternoon, the neatly laid out rows of graves, mostly of Englishmen who had died during the last war, were particularly poignant here in hot

African sunlight, so far from home. They found one of a young air force lad, killed at 19, with a small bunch of artificial poppies in a jar in front of it. They took a photo and later through a British legion, Charlie found the address of the boy's mother and sent it to her as proof that the yearly gift to her son was actually received.

They all had a good time and the holiday worked for both of them. He was trying to make amends. And since both partners really wanted to still try, they were eventually successful. Charlie accepted reluctantly that his life for better or worse, was now set. There would be no magic awakening; there was nothing waiting around the corner; there never would be that one special dream person that he could open his very soul to, and pour his love and care into, and he would never have a child now of his own. When he had first met Kat it hadn't seemed important; his experiences with her lads had been difficult, to say the least, but here in his mid-forties, the awakening of the fact that now it could never happen, and what he had missed out on through his own choice caused him deep regret.

What he had got was what it would be; Kat loved him dearly, but possessively and overwhelmingly. He had money, position and even a bit of prestige. He loathed the thought of becoming 50 but that was still five years off. He had been proposed as a local magistrate. There were still happy things, satisfying things that he could enjoy and do, but there would now always be this sense of unfulfillment emotionally, something empty, that he knew he had missed in his life, but this was it, his life, Kat's life, whatever he had hoped it would be, nothing was going to change now.

He was bitterly disappointed that for him, it had never been possible to maintain the early feelings he felt when he was in love; he longed to recapture that excitement; his first love, she had filled his life for four years, then left him, that had been adolescence, but she had stayed in his mind for years afterwards her rejection had hurt him emotionally, but at that age, no real damage was done. That was the first time he knew love though, and the way it ended had shattered him. He had felt it again but differently in his late 20s with the one he remembered as the big love of his life, Maureen, but with her, it was almost an unrequited love, strictly one-sided on his behalf and a fact they had only gone to bed once and that near the end of their relationship, he had tried and tried to win her for nearly three years but she had been the one and only failure that he really ever wanted; she had cried when she told him she was marrying someone else, but Charlie was young then.

When you can roll with it in the sure certainty that there will be someone else, and there had been, still it had given him misery at the time and she also stayed in his mind for years; with both of them, it had lasted as strongly from the beginning to the end. Both times he had been hurt and so he had known and felt for both Tracey and Kat when they, in turn, were hurt by him, and it had made it nearly impossible for him to break from them. With Tracey, it had been for Kat, their feelings for each other had been the only thing that made it possible. With Kat now that there never would be anyone else, it had just developed into two people who were so used to each other that the idea of leaving her and starting on his own again was unthinkable, even the mental frustration could be lined with; *just don't listen* became his watchword. They were still good for each other in many other ways.

Once again, did it really matter that he could no longer be excited by sex with her? *How many times do you enjoy eating lobster* became his axiom; yes, it had been great again with Bella. He had memories of that and they were all sexual nothing else, but the reality was never going to live up to the desires, and looking at his physical self now, he knew he was never going to attract that one special person, middle age would be followed by old age, ce la vie.

At about this time, his association with the new company that had been formed when he sold the family firm came to an end. His friend Aidan had invested a lot of money into this. Charlie had warned him time and again not to waste so much, but he had junior partner Jordan, who was actually the one involved at street level and seemed to think that if they pumped enough in, they would be buying success. Aidan would say that he only wanted to be involved provided Charlie ran it.

Jordan would then go and spend more money and in the end, when the bank started to squeeze them, Jordan panicked. The difficulties in reconciling the solicitor's mentality in business with that of the estate agent's urgency in sales proved unsurmountable. Charlie had been overpaid, and it just wasn't on, to go on taking money from friends, so one day, he cleaned out his desk in the office he had worked in for over 20 years, with all its memories and associations, went to see Aidan at his home, told him once and for all that it couldn't work, advised him to sell as quickly as possible and went home to run his hotel.

Chapter 13
The Revived 45

Three months later, he saw a manager's job advertised in a company he knew and entered the final phase of his life. He enjoyed the challenges; he had worried that he might not be able to keep up with the younger salesman and the latest techniques. He soon found out that there was nothing to worry about. They were easy meat to him and there were no new techniques at all, only the old ones that he had cut his teeth on, that they just thought they were new. There were strong rumours that the company was going to be bought by the Nationwide Agency chain and an apprehensive Charlie took his fears to his friend Jordan, the partner in the back office who assured him there was no plan at all, and that he had no cause for any alarm; no way were they going to sell to the nationwide or anyone else.

Reassured, Charlie got on with building up the sales and that month actually won the much-hyped sales competitions for the second time; his office had never been first in its whole history before and he did without cheating. One month later, the company was sold; that was the end of all trust or care between Charlie and his 'friends'; after that, he only did what he wanted and in the way that suited him. He started to do deals again, anything cheap that came onto the market he would first offer to his specials, all who cut him in on the profit got the first choice and these together with his wage and commission plus the fact that having his hotel which gave him a completely free living, meant in real terms that he was earning well in excess of £30,000 a year/*this would be equivalent to 115k by today's standards/*. Never did any outright crooked deals, he just bent the rules.

He had no reason to do otherwise as he was comfortably secure, had all the material possessions he could want and knew that he would eventually inherit his family's money. He and Kat treated themselves to a very expensive holiday, a cruise on the Nile, with their two friends again. Cairo was a terrible dump, vastly overcrowded, stinking hot, dirty and smelly, but the Pyramids were magic, vast and solid they had been there forever. Charlie climbed the inside of the main one, only to find after all the effort, one empty tomb, but the ancient stones had a feel all of their own; his favourite was one where the architects had got the sums wrong, it was called the collapsed pyramid for obvious reasons. He had great sympathy for that one; he knew in advance from all his family who had been to Egypt in the war that all Egyptians were dirty, cowardly thieves who would stab you as soon as they looked at you.

What he found were some of the friendliest people in the world. He went to the main museum and saw Tutankhamen in all his glory; the guide apologised that Nefertiti was on loan, and Charlie laughed because he had already seen her in Berlin. He looked at the world's original condoms, linen sheaths impregnated with oil, with thongs around the back. He learnt very quickly how hieroglyphics could be read; you only needed to remember a few key signs for the rest to make sense.

They cruised down to Luxor and as he sat one evening watching the ancient Nile flow past looking up at the jet-black sky, pierced by a million stars, feeling the warmth of the night under the palm trees, he enjoyed a feeling of timelessness and inner peace. He didn't feel it for long though, because in spite of all the precautions he had taken, later that night, he came down with the dreaded Egyptian curse. Normally, this left you feeling close to death and Charlie's case was just the same, but here he was having come all this way ready to go and see the Valley of the Kings, no way was he going to miss that.

The trouble with sightseeing in Egypt was that the sun was so hot by mid-morning that tours had to start very early to avoid heat stroke. This one started at 6 a.m. and so literally having girded up his loins, he forced himself at dawn to walk through what felt like the valley of the shadow of death he never regretted it. The history of these ancient kings and queens unfolded before him; the wall pictures and paintings in the deepest tombs all told of the journey from this life to the next, the fertility symbols, the gods of life and death, all clearly seen as on the day they were first painted, thousands of years before.

They enjoyed a performance of son et Lumiere in the temples of Karnak, and saw the huge figures at Abu Simbel, moved intact by modern technology to a higher position where once a year on the pharaoh's birthday, the shaft of sunlight penetrated the entire length of the tomb and lit up the face of his statue; how was it possible to plan that—incredible.

Back home again, life went on. There were no immediate changes at work after the sell-out; there were no changes at home either. Kat's daughter Daphne married for the second time in three years and fell pregnant on her honeymoon. Her new husband was no better or worse than all the other men she had known. She was still going for looks rather than anything else and seemed incapable of settling with anyone for long; each new one was the 'one and only' for a few months, then she seemed able to discard them at will, have a couple of weeks of tears, then get on with the next; none of her men seemed to care too much. The only one in fact who was visibly hurt was a young Jewish boy called Tyler, he had promptly emigrated to South Africa, where to Charlie's astonishment, he joined the police force and transformed from an intelligent rather sensitive young man into a bigoted neo-Nazi.

Charlie still had stirrings from time to time. A young blonde divorcee in their mortgage and finance department seemed to respond favourably but he knew she had been involved with two of his fellow managers so he never tried to follow it up. She eventually got engaged to one of the 19-year-old juniors. She was 27 with a young child. Charlie felt only sorrow for her for making yet another mistake. And so, the stage was set, the actors were all in their places and the final chapter inexorably unrolled, everything in his whole life pointed him in one direction only, fate had shown his hand a last.

Chapter 14
The Impossible Dream

Sunday mornings became a pleasure for Charlie, the highlight of his week in many ways. At first, he and Bridget took turns showing Mia—the new girl the ropes, but Charlie took to going in just because he wanted to. It did in fact make Mondays easier if he could get his work ready beforehand. And it was nice to have a lie-in and then pop in for a coffee and chat and spend an hour or so getting things organised. Mia was an eager learner; she was quick and organised and always willing to do extra hours to help out. And she had the touch; anyone can be an estate agent once you have learnt the basics, but without that certain something, you will never be anything special in the trade.

Bridget hadn't got it; Kat had and so did Mia. She had started in March and doing only one short session a week; she had made her first sale in just over a month. The office was quite busy in those days, but in between lulls, she and Charlie would talk at first generally, and then personally, he became fascinated by her. She had so much potential stored up in her; he wanted to help her develop it to its full. He thought she was lovely to look at; he could see of course that she was receptive to him, but he was quite positive that it was only her friendly attitude, and how could there be anything else?

She could have her pick of men, what on earth did he imagine she could possibly want from him, lovely idea, but preposterous. He asked her what the high point of her week had been; she said that apart from coming here to the office, it had been shopping at Waitrose. She told him that she had two little girls, one of five; the other just over two. Her husband, whose name she never mentioned looked after them whilst she was at work; he was a store manager for Dickens & Jones's at Seven Sisters. She had been born in South London to Irish Catholic parents, who had moved back to Ireland when she was 16. She had gone with them but hated it; she met her husband there when they both worked for D&J and after they were married, she converted to his Jewish faith.

She said she never felt Jewish, and that she had never been a believing Catholic. At that time, she was 28, had been married for five years; her husband was 12 years older and was very overweight, in spite of her efforts to get him to diet, he was slightly shorter than Charlie, but weighed some 16 stone. The thought of the two of them in bed together was most repugnant to Charlie. One weekday, she brought her little girls in for a visit; he was captured by them. Olivia the smallest was so shy, clinging to her mother's skirts, until Charlie remembered he had a glove puppet in his drawer—it was Kermit and she loved it.

At home, things with Kat were no better or worse than for a long time. Daphne had given birth to Sophia, his goddaughter, but within three months, her husband had gone. Beatrix married for the fifth time, after a gap of 15 years, and she lived in Spain with her new husband. Charlie disliked Spain but Kat prevailed upon him to take her there for a few days to stay with them; reluctantly, he agreed, and then occurred the first of what become repeated and unaccountable coincidences with Mia.

He was clearing his work on Saturday morning ready to fly out in the late afternoon. He started to write a memo to Mia for the next day, his thoughts dwelling more and more on her as he did so, and so it developed into a more personal note, telling her that in some ways since he really didn't want to go, he would miss their Sunday morning together. At that moment, she walked into the office straight from the hairdressers and looked absolutely gorgeous. He gave her the note and they laughed at the timing; she said she had just called in to wish him a happy holiday, but her smiles seemed to be more than just friendly. She said she too would miss him, and his mind became a turmoil, surely it could be anything really; she was putting out, for god's sake, he was 18 years older than her, and look at him, he was just imagining things because he wanted to so much.

Spain was fun in some respects. Charlie and Kat had not been together for over two months. They tried it once whilst they were away, little knowing that it would be for the last time; it was perfunctory and neither of them got any real enjoyment from it. Sitting alone on the terrace, gazing at the mountains, Charlie's mind was on Mia. He seemed to be talking to her inside his head if only it were true he thought, but she was beyond his wildest dreams. When they returned, nothing had changed on the surface, but in last June, he asked Mia if she would like a lunchtime drink one Saturday.

They went to a local favourite pub and just talked together; he asked her if she could get an evening off one night and have dinner with him; this seemed to surprise and fluster her, so he dropped the subject. She told him of the difficulties she had with her mother-in-law, a woman whose every whim her son had to obey or risk a family split on the one and only time she had stood up for herself she had been made to apologise. Her new job had opened her horizons and she was happier and more relaxed than she had been for years.

In July, Charlie's office nearly won the sales competition and he decided that they would celebrate anyway; he would pay for it himself this time. It would make a nice evening out for all of them. The others all went in one car. He picked up Mia outside his local and after a hurried drink, he had been late arriving. They joined up together at his favourite Italian restaurant in Hoxton. This also was owned by a friend of his and they got the usual attentive service. Charlie sat next to Mia, but the conversation flowed between them all; as they said goodnight, he kissed the other girls in his perfectly natural way and then he dropped Mia back to her car. They sat and talked for a few minutes; she told him it had been simply ages since she had been out to dinner thanked him and got out to leave.

Charlie placed his hands on her shoulders lightly and bent to kiss her goodnight; his ordinary little pack lasted about three seconds when she opened her lips and kissed him back passionately for what seemed like minutes. He was totally mind-blowingly amazed. It could not possibly conceivably be happening. They clung to each other there in the car park. He was a complete loss for words. "Are you surprised?" She asked getting back into his car.

They repeated the exercise this time with him fully participating; he had never ever felt such a feeling of emotion just from one kiss. He answered her question as best he could; surprise, yes, of course, he had wanted her for weeks, but had thought it impossible that she would fancy him. The following day, he phoned her; she said she was literally climbing the walls, *where had I heard that before? H*e thought. On Saturday, she called into the office with her children. In front of the others, it was impossible to make more than eye contact, but in conversation, he told her he was staying in that night. He had got a decent video ordered and would have a quiet evening after work. As he went to collect his film who should be accidentally there again with the kids no privacy was possible. He mentioned he would be taking his dogs for a walk in the park. They met halfway inside and walked slowly around the familiar paths he had taken so many times before. He had the dogs to keep his eye on; she had her girls; they could not even touch for a moment in front of the children but as they sat on the grass, their fingertips found each other is it each other's.

The next day being a Sunday, he raced to the office to see how they embraced kissing each other passionately, clinging to each other; she said over and over, "This will never be enough for you. I know you will get fed up with it soon. I want so much to give you more but I just can't." He reassured her it was wonderful; it was enough it had to be meaningful and knowing it to be true.

On Tuesday, they arranged to meet for lunch; she said, "Don't bother with lunch; it will take up too much of our precious hour." They met in the same place, drove down the road to the forest and parked in the first available place kissing and holding each other oblivious to passing traffic. She had bought three times as much as they could eat; he thought she must have believed she was catching for her husband. This went on for some three weeks; sometimes she would be in her bright red Peugeot; sometimes in her husband's grey Toyota. She was strictly regulated by her girls' school times. Olivia had just started playschool from 11:50, whilst Charlotte was there until 3:00.

On one of their first lunches, they began to really talk together as a private couple. She told him she would never leave her husband and that the children came first in her life. He explored her body from the outside; she accidentally on purpose dropped her hand into his lap when he was aroused apologising at once and saying it had been a mistake. They talked for hours on the phone. He soon discovered every phone booth in the area; she would follow him around on his appointments waiting for Olivia to fall asleep, so they could be together in one car whilst they could watch her from his. Their embraces became more and more passionate.

And then the time came for her to go on holiday with her husband. They both hated separation and she would find excuses to sleep away just to ring him at night. Kat became suspicious of these calls because Charlie had never answered the phone so quickly in his life. She had gone to the West Country; by coincidence, Charlie's mother was down there at the same time and they were staying in adjacent hotels in Torquay. One of her calls came during a fire trail with an impossible dialogue on as he pretended that he was answering a genuine inquiry. Bells were shrilling, people everywhere and all he wanted to hear was the sound of her voice and she, his. When she returned, he realised that the break had been almost more than he could bear and he told her he was in love with her.

Chapter 15
At All Costs

At home, he was in a hell of a state withdrawing from contact with Kat. It was cruel and he hated himself for doing it, but Mia filled his every moment. For the first time, their marriage was in real danger and she sensed it immediately fighting back as best she knew how. But after all the years of disillusionment and frustration, there just was not enough to hold him now. He withdrew into himself as well and it only made things worse for her—the more she tried. He was confused and worried, he knew his feelings were alright but Mia was quite definite about not leaving her home and after all, apart from his own feelings nothing much had happened just emotionally.

One morning before 9:00 a.m. as he took Kat to her office, he saw Mia parked on the corner watching him. She had taken to driving past his hotel; he in turn would find any excuse to drive around her house. He had to be more than careful because she lived in a very nice detached home on the private estate next door; in fact, to one of his fellow Rotarians.

One morning, he called unexpectedly to her house at about 10:30. She met him in her dressing gown and it was obvious she had still been in bed. Olivia was there so nothing could develop; this was only the second time he had been there; the first time was when he gave her a free valuation. He remembered following her jeans-clad figure upstairs and being shown every room in the house. They once spent two hours clinging to each other in an empty ex-council flat in Fairfield court. They went to a furnished flat in Woodley one afternoon just for ten minutes together; this stretched into over half an hour, which caused both of them much concern.

She had left both the girls in her car parked outside the window, where they could keep their eye on them, but she had Charlie got carried away with each other and when she returned, both the kids were crying and in a state, they both swore they would never let the girls be harmed that way again. One night, Charlotte had an asthma attack that caused her to spend the night in the hospital. Charlie knew nothing about it until the next day, but when Mia told him she had driven past his home just hoping to see him and tell him and then spent the night on a camp bed; he felt hurt and useless.

She had needed him and he couldn't have got away to help her because of his still living with Kat. The next time they went to Woodley, they had more time. He began to explore her fully for the first time; she wanted him to but told him she was shy of him looking at her. She, however, definitely wanted to look at him staring at the belt on his trousers until she beheld his pride and joy for the first time. As usual, it was a most impressive sight for a woman but all too soon, they had to leave. As they were going back to the car, she said in a quiet little voice that she did in fact love him. *What a moment to pick* he thought, *why couldn't she have said so ten minutes earlier?*

The rest of the days passed in amazing time until their next possible date. It was now late August and Charlie had the whole afternoon off. She had made arrangements for the girls and she prepared a lovely picnic. He drove her out to the country to show her the cottage he had lived in for so many years, and then a corn field that he had played in as a boy. They spread the blanket on the ground and the tree that he used to climb and play in and for the first time discovered each other's bodies. There could be nothing further, as she had her period, but it was a fabulous afternoon nonetheless. She told him again that she loved him; she undid him completely and then pulled her own dress off they drank wine, ate smoked salmon, talked and fondled each other. She expressed her desire to sit on top of him and told him she needed a lot of loving. This concerned him immediately as he had not expected them to actually go further than they had. He doubted very much that he would be good enough for her, but she was so lovely to look at, that he determined to try and hoped for the best.

She gave him his first present a D&J tie that she had chosen for him. She mentioned that she made her husband use condoms as she couldn't go on the pill. This worried Charlie as well. He hadn't used one in years and had never liked them. That weekend, there was an old Neil Diamond film on the TV; they discovered a mutual love for this. Part of the story shows a non-Jewish girl being taught the religious rituals. Mia said she would enjoy teaching Charlie how to do this for the girls; they discovered that they must have been sitting almost opposite each other at the Neil

Diamond concert a couple of years earlier and his records became a mutual feeling between them.

Rosha Shona came, and Charlie felt completely left out the thought of the whole finally going to the Synagogue together filled him with envy as he conjured up mental pictures of them there; typically though her husband could not be bothered to go. Mia told him that she was perfectly prepared to bring up the girls in her husband's faith but only if he would make the effort himself. She had converted because she had promised to, but it had made little or no difference to his family; she didn't feel Jewish herself and in fact, she had no religious belief at all. She felt only that what parts of you that went into your children would leave on after you were dead.

13 September was her birthday; her husband took her to dinner in the Bijou Restaurant but no sooner had they returned home and he had gone to bed that she was on the phone to Charlie. Kat had also gone to bed but it only needed one or the other to pick up an extension. Mia had started an evening course in typing at a local school. They would meet for ten minutes beforehand and half an hour afterwards parking either under the bridge or in the Marcus Square—a very dark secluded car park.

One day, Charlie had driven his mother down to Hove to stay with her sister for a few days. He spoke to Mia on the phone in the afternoon and came home on the train thinking constantly about her. As he stepped out of Woodward station, she was waiting to surprise him. They clung together both bursting with their emotions. At the end of the first week in September, events overtook them at last. Kat overheard Charlie talking on the phone, confronted him with it and a huge row took place. She left home there and then to stay with her daughter Daphne. Her second marriage had gone the way of her first and she was living alone in a maisonette in Luton with her baby. Shortly before this, Mia had gone down to her parents' home in Shoreham for a break. The children were left with their father overnight. Charlie had the afternoon off and on the pretext of Rotary business told Kat he would be out until about 11:30. He met Mia in the car park at the Carrington Hotel in East Uckfield, a place that had many happy old memories. She arrived about 7:30 driving her husband's car.

Charlie told her he had booked a room where they could be alone together in comfort for the first time. This took her by surprise, and they had a drink whilst she thought about it. He convinced her that he really wasn't expecting anything else other than what they had already enjoyed with each other. He really did mean it that way too because he was frightened that he would disappoint her if he took it further. She finished her drink and said, "Come on then, let's not waste any more time."

It was one of the most wonderful times of Charlie's life; they closed and locked the door and all alone together at last. She was wearing a long peach-coloured skirt which creased alarmingly; they lay in their underwear on the bed kissing and caressing, Charlie kept his shirt on because he was afraid that she would be put off by his overweight figure. She laughed and said, "It looks lovely to me; you should see what I'm used to."

Later, she went to the bathroom and when she emerged, he saw her completely naked for the first time with the light shining behind him through a whole tangle of golden curls;

she was the most beautiful vision he had ever seen. They did not make love. She pulled back at the last minute and said no matter how much she wanted to, she would never be able to look her husband in the eye again. They lay together talking and smoking and he asked her about her early life and lovers.

The answers she gave him honestly appalled and amazed him for he was so much infatuated by her that the stories she told him then nearly made him cry. There she lay in his arms beautiful and vulnerable, telling him she had lost her virginity at 14½ to a musician friend of her fathers. Because of pressures at 16, she was involved with a sailor; she didn't enjoy it with either of them. She had met her husband in Dublin when she was 19 senior sales assistant at D&J. He had been an assistant manager 12 years older than her; there had been nothing except sex between them for the first two years. He was totally obsessed with sex in every facet. She looked upon him as the only real man she had ever known.

The choice of Irish boys left her cold; she said he was the only man who had ever given her an orgasm and that the two of them had practised every position known in the book anywhere and everywhere. He would bring a whole real hard-core magazine and the most explicit adult videos. He would masturbate literally for hours and he had a preference for using cucumbers on her. She built a good picture of him as a gross, perverted, totally selfish pig. She told him that as the two years came to an end, and she knew he would be transferred back to England, she had no intention of being left behind, but his family would never approve of him marrying out of faith.

They went on holiday to Rhodes; neither of them taking any precautions playing Russian roulette as she put it and Charlotte was conceived whilst she was standing on her head. Charlie's head was spinning; he wanted to hold her and protect her for the rest of his life, but he was scared stiff of ever trying to consume their own relationship. How could he ever follow that?

His final memory of the evening was of Mia sitting naked with her arm crossed over her knee up against the head foot of the bed smoking a cigarette deep in thought wearing only her gold necklace chain. That vision would remain in his mind forever; of course, they had overdone it. They left at midnight and Charlie knew he would not be home before 1:30; how in hell's name was he going to explain that? Maybe he could get away by saying he had a breakdown. He needn't have bothered because thrashing his Mercedes back down the motorway five miles from Woodward, he did in fact break down for the very first time. Consequently, it was 3.30 before he eventually arrived with a genuine ironside alibi; a night to remember, all alright.

Chapter 16
The Miracle Worker

Kat's leaving opened the floodgates for the two of them. On one of his afternoons off, Charlie was passing the kitchen window, when he noticed a girl walking past on the other side of the road. His eyesight was poor at that distance; what he noticed first was that she had a walk identical to Mia's distinctive one. As she came closer, his heart skipped a bit because it was of course Mia herself. He asked her in for a coffee, introduced her to his very suspicious mother and they set and played an innocent game of cards; neither of them could possibly concentrate. But the ice had been broken.

Kat in her anguish was phoning everyone she knew looking for support and understanding. She found Bridget, who not wishing to become involved and took the accusation to Charlie's boss Jordan. The next day, Charlie spent a very difficult time calming things down and denying the truth. His mother and he had a huge row when he said if Mia wanted to call round, it was his home and if he welcomed her, it was just too bad. Kat's leaving meant Mia could now ring at any time and the two of them talked at length every day and evening. Snatching whatever times, they could when they could; late in the month, Charlie was instructed to sell an empty house on Fairfield Road just a few doors away from where he knew Bella was still living. Another coincidence?

One room was still carpeted and had a leather-red armchair in it. He and Mia went there one Saturday after work; they were both completely undressed; nothing else was likely to happen when Mia gave a deep groan and said, "I want you now." She lay back on the carpet ready. But the horror of horrors, Charlie had left the condoms in the car; by the time he could dress, run down to the car, back again and undress again, the moment had passed but they both now knew that next time they had the opportunity, there would be no turning back.

By a stroke of luck, their next time together was a lovely late warm sunny day. Mia had packed a picnic basket and they drove to their field again. This time, they went further in. Charlie carried her across a footbridge and deeper into the field; it was by the riverbank where he had played as a lad and where years before in his teens, he had taken Jade, his first love for a kiss and a cuddle. It was full of happy memories and seemed totally right for this occasion that they had been waiting for so long. It was to Charlie as if the place itself had been waiting for him for just this time. Mia, he knew was the last final love of his life; the one elusive dream that he had never thought would come this late, the place was right, the time was right, and would he be right as well? He wasn't.

They spread their blanket, undressed each other completely, and there in the peace and tranquilly of the countryside, he knew so well, he blew it, by the time she had squeezed him into a too-small condom, he couldn't last 30 seconds. They ate their lunch, drank some wine and tried again. This time, he managed a little better, but at the crucial moment, a light aeroplane flew low overhead obviously sporting what was going on it refused to go away circling above them. Charlie gave it the V-sign, and Mia in a totally instinctive way, covered not her body, which might have been expected but her face, it wasn't spoilt for them but Charlie knew that it had been a real let down for Mia; her first man other than her husband she had been with for seven years.

One of Charlie's deals was a tatty old house in West Grove. He had the keys it had a bed and it was safe; he had sold it to Aidan, no one would bother them there, but it was hardly romantic.

They started to go there at every opportunity; gradually, he improved and he nearly made it several times. He borrowed the keys to his friend Callum's flat. Mia had prepared thoroughly wearing the most sensual black underwear, but this time, Charlie failed miserably; whatever she tried, he was unable to get started; angry, frustrated and bitterly disappointed, he knew it was the end of his dream; not only could he not satisfy her he was worse than useless. He told Mia that this was the finish for them as he just couldn't manage anymore, he was too old and that was it.

She cried and told him no; it didn't matter together they would get it right. He made her promise never to fake it; if she did, he would never know. He resolved immediately to get medical help. He went privately to see an old Rotary doctor friend. When he came out, Mia was waiting as a surprise; he told her that his friend was fixing for him to see a specialist. Olivia was with her and together, they collected conkers and took her to the local KFC. Charlie had met her 19-year-old sister, Harper; by this time, a girl who immediately took a strong liking to, the first time had been in the office. Then one night, she and Mia went out for a drink and rang Charlie from the local horrible pub. Kat was still at home then, but he made some excuse or other and rushed to meet them.

One of the regulars was having a birthday drink; his wife had arranged for a stripogram. Both girls were fascinated by this; the stripper was an old boiler. She undressed her victim down to his underpants and there he stood, white and with his beer gut hanging out and his paisley socks, a fine figure of a man. The following weekend, Harper brought a friend with her, and Charlie took all three to the country club; the younger girls loved the disco, but since Harper knew nothing of their relationship, it was totally frustrating there was no privacy at all. Mia was waiting outside the gent's toilet and when Charlie came out, she embraced him passionately for a few seconds. Harper professed that she was still a virgin at 19, she said when she died, they would put 'returned unopened' on her grave.

Late in the month, Charlie had to attend a computer course in Northampton. He and Bridget together with a couple from another office drove there on Sunday evening. Charlie had absolutely no experience at all with computers; he was dreading the bloody things. He had no photos of Mia at all and he asked her for something nice and sexy, to take with him; at that time, she was getting rid of dozens that her husband had taken, but what she chose to give him shocked him, but excited him at the same time. One was of her sprawled naked across the chair, obviously immediately after intercourse, one was of her naked except for dark stockings and high-heeled shoes, showing her lower anatomy in full detail, but the one that really perturbed him, was one of her fingering herself, she said they were the pick of the bunch, as she didn't think he would want anything with cucumbers sticking out. The course was a waste of time for Charlie, except that he gained some familiarity with the system.

Mia had phoned him before breakfast time, unheard of for her to be awake at that time of day. She wished him luck and told him to hurry back. On the return journey, he and Bridget talked together very personally, she told him of her early lovers, and how she had married her husband because of his looks; she had borne a child, who was dead at birth, and after that, there was nothing left of her feelings for him. A former lover who she had left because he wouldn't marry her came back on the scene, and one day, she left a letter and ran off with him to Ireland. She was there for two years on an isolated farm; her lover still wouldn't marry her and it just didn't work. She fell pregnant again and he told her to get rid of it. So, she came to her parents, they being good Catholics decided that their shame in front of the neighbours would be too great, and so she did in fact have an abortion.

She had chosen Padraig her fiancée not because she loved him, but because she knew she could rely on him totally. Charlie, in turn, confessed to her about Mia totally. She had guessed as much of course, and he told her of his sexual problems and hang-ups with her—it cemented their friendship deeply.

The firm's sports night was shortly after this. Mia called at Charlie's hotel first and they made love in one of the empty bedrooms; his mother was away at the time. He gave her first orgasm that night, but orally, which she loved; by now, she had taught him the movements that she needed, 'pushing the right buttons' she called it. Eventually, the two of them made a token appearance at the do; driving back she put her arm around him, sending tingles down his spine, she had phoned her husband earlier to check on the kids.

When they parted, Charlie felt so lonely, he wondered how much longer they could go on like this, ecstatic when they were together, miserable after every parting. They were meeting every single day now, but never for long enough. One Sunday lunchtime when he had roused her but they had not been able to do anything further about it, she had gone home and spent the afternoon in bed with her husband; she blamed Charlie for it and said she had been fantasising him whilst she did it. They booked into the Grove Hotel for the first time arriving at 12 and leaving at 3; bathing together, she introduced him to her speciality 'ball wash'; it really was very special indeed. He had been seeing his sexual specialist who had taken the most embarrassing tests, and who had cost several hundred pounds, but he reassured Charlie that there was no physical problem, most of it lay in his mind, just remember that at his age turning it on at all odd hours and in the oddest places was bound to cause difficulties for him.

They discovered The Palace Hotel in Barking and had one of their very best sessions on Thursday. He still felt that every time he kissed her or made love to her, it could be for the last time. She had written a letter to him telling him of her hopes and desires for the two of them, but reminding him that children were her life. One afternoon when she called the office, he felt so hurt by their parting that he told her he was at the end of his tether. They just could not go on.

A couple of days later, they were sitting under the arches; Ollie was asleep in her car parked outside and Mia seemed to come to some sort of decision herself. "Ok," she said, "now how do we go on about it?" Charlie told her that come what may, her future and that of the girls would be safe forever with him; that he felt he had been waiting and hoping for her for years and that he had never had such depth of feeling in his life before. She expressed her wish to work with him in a business of her own either as an estate agent or hotel and they started to plan the future together.

She grew more careless with her meetings, saying she no longer cared; it was as if she was goading her husband to find out. She took the children down to her parents and wrote Charlie the most beautiful letter saying why she loved him. He had said to her that he just couldn't imagine what she saw in him a middle-aged overweight, wig-wearing bore. She had laughed and cheekily poked him on the hairpiece; now in this, letter she told him, she said that her husband was just finishing the most important job of his career, it would take about three weeks and she owed it to him not to make the break until he had finished. She said that her only fear was that she and the girls may be left on their own if it didn't work out.

On the second of November, she came down to the hotel at about 10 p.m. She told Charlie that her husband Ramiro, she had finally named him, something she had never done before, had come home and gone to bed, that she couldn't stay away a minute longer and she didn't care if he woke up or not. They sat in Ramiro's car this time, sipping at vodka and tonics, talking and watching the rain on the windscreen. She dropped him off at about 11.30 p.m. As he walked into his lounge, the phone was ringing. It was Ramiro, waking to find his wife gone; he thought she might be doing some typing for Charlie. She had been doing some of his Rotary work, which gave them an excuse to meet. Charlie was non-committal, knowing she would arrive back any moment. He stalled Ramiro for time; sure enough, he heard her arrive. He did not phone her the next day, or evening. Obviously, something was taking place; she would ring him if there was real trouble, so he might make matters even worse by trying to contact her. He drove past her house eight or nine times; both cars were parked outside, so it was obvious that there was something serious going on.

Charlie felt desperate and helpless. That evening, he answered the front door to be met by a hulking figure. It was Ramiro; they had never seen each other before; he was controlling his fury as best he could. His little piggy eyes were nearly popping out of his head. Charlie knew he was in real physical danger, he could not of course back down, and so he faced up to it and invited him in. Ramiro sat there glowering at him, not knowing what Mia might have confessed; he was at a loss to know what he should say himself. Ramiro demanded to know if his intentions were serious, in answer to, 'Will you marry her?'

Charlie replied from his heart, "Yes, tomorrow if it was possible."

He told Ramiro that the children would be safe in his protection and that he would see that they were always available to him. And that as far as he was concerned if there was a divorce; he would see that any financial settlement would be eased for him. Charlie told him frankly that he was more than able to provide for Mia and the girls.

The next day, Mia rang from the Grove Hotel—she had left her home after hours and hours of conflict, finally admitting she was involved with Charlie. Ramiro had been on the phone to her father and he had come racing up to their home. She told Charlie that they were out for his blood and that she had left rather than face him. Charlie expected any minute to be invaded and had prepared himself for the worst. But nothing happened; he called Mia's hotel at the earliest moment and then went to his own hotel to see if there had been any developments. There had; Ramiro had been on the phone to Charlie's mother, pleading his case, how Charlie had smashed up his happy little family. She of course agreed and an almighty row ensured; Charlie left and joined Mia at the Grove.

She had brought nothing with her except framed photos of the girls, which she had placed on the bedside table. They talked for hours reassuring each other and calming each other down. Later, they made love and Charlie left at dawn.

Mia avoided seeing her father. Ramiro demanded to see Charlie again and they met in the local pub. He told Charlie that Mia's father would cut her off from the entire family unless she agreed there and then to stop the affair. Eventually, Mia did go down to her parents and after the most miserable days he could ever remember, she rang him to say she had agreed to go back to her husband. And her father had phoned him to tell him so. Charlie was shattered, but he could understand the pressure and tried to reassure her that she was doing the right thing. He walked around the park alone with his dogs for hours; he had lost her what sort of marriage would she have now? How much damage have they done? Her sister Harper phoned him and implied that all was not yet lost.

Mia had been crying for days, but Harper knew how determined she could be when she wanted something. Shortly afterwards Mia came back to Woodward, she called Charlie's home that evening, but he was out; she had talked to his mother in tears, saying, "I love him; I cannot live without him, but I have to go back to my husband for the children's sake." His mother warned her of the damage that she would do to Charlie if she hurt him further, at his age, and with his intensity, he would never recover if it went wrong.

And so, Mia returned to the matrimonial fold. When Charlie arrived home, his mother told him to be prepared for the worst. Mia had said she would come back later that night to tell him herself. And say goodbye. He waited, getting himself braced for the ordeal, deciding that somehow, he would have to make it as easy for her as possible. But sick inside at the thought of losing this, his one great last chance of love. By the time she came, he had calmed himself and was waiting for the inevitable. He heard her arrive and called her upstairs to the privacy of his room. As she entered, he held out his arms and said, "It's all right, my love, I understand that this is how it will have to be." She was white as a sheet; he hadn't seen her for days, and her vulnerability pierced him through and through. She smiled weakly and uttered the words that would change all their lives, "Who says I am going to leave you?" She said clinging to him. "I had to make that promise under pressure." From that moment on, they were both lost.

Chapter 17
Humble Beginnings

For her husband, it was ruin; she had chosen just one day before his grand opening at work, the worst possible timing for him. And he broke immediately, sent back home by his employers. He was literally unable to function. All day and every day, he hammered at Mia, trying to make her change her mind. He turned to threats, he would send copies of their explicit home videos to everyone connected, and he would kill both her and Charlie. He sat playing with a dagger, saying five years in prison would be well worth it. Each time she fled the home, Charlie would be there to comfort her and protect her; it turned into physical violence between them and the idea of her little size 10 body fighting great bulk filled Charlie with horror.

On one occasion, she had to call Charlotte her eldest into the room in order to make him stop; she could not come to stay with Charlie because of the children, so she stuck it out at her home. Charlie rented an unfurnished flat in Seven Kings with his friend Callum just as an emergency bolt hole. Ramiro would rush round to neighbours to have Poloride pictures taken of his 'injuries'; the police were involved. By another quirk of fate, this involved Kat's daughter, Daphne, who was in charge of matrimonial dispute units locally.

Together, Charlie and Mia grabbed what few hours together that they could, but each parting filled him with sorrows. He would gaze after her departing car watching it as long as he could. She would phone him ceaselessly. The Christmas holidays were approaching; it would be Mia's first Christmas in years; her mother-in-law would have caused too much of a scene, being Jewish so it would be the first one ever for the girls. Mia would be taking them to her parents, first though she brought them to Charlie's hotel for tea, the two of them had been out shopping. Mia introduced Charlie to Brentwood Centre and he bought a globe of the world for Charlotte and a snowman doll for Ollie.

His mother made a special effort together with his widowed Aunt Betty. They had gone to a lot of trouble to get this little party together. It was the first chance to break the ice and Charlie loved it. They discovered a motel at Brentwood not very nice, but quite cheap and obviously safe for them. On their second visit there, they booked for the morning and then went back again in the evening. Mia by now was having some difficulties of her own. Charlie at full strength really was nearly more than she could comfortably manage, and she had been to the chemists to obtain some cream.

The coldness of this gave Charlie an entirely new sensation and they very nearly wore each other out. Once again, they made full use of the bath. Mia told him that she still had a great fear of AIDS. They had talked about it at length beforehand; she said that she really wanted to have a full sexual relationship with him now, implying that he needed to prove that he was clear; at this late stage, he couldn't see much point in this, and he never was quite sure what she was talking about.

Mia came back alone for the office party; they left early and booked into the Boat House; she was wearing a brand-new red dress and for once, she was wearing make-up. She looked a million dollars; by far the most attractive girl in the company. Later that night, he drove her down to Haywards Heath.

They parked for a while and said lingering goodbye. Charlie drove all the way home alone, for him, Christmas was already over.

Ramiro had gone to the Canary Islands with his sister and brother-in-law. No sooner had he returned than D&J booked him into a health farm. Mia had a real fear of being alone in the house at night. For nearly two years after Olivia was born, she had suffered from what she called her 'phobia' ceaselessly roaming the house for up to hours every night, checking and rechecking the windows and doors. Ramiro had made appointments for her to see psychiatrists, but she would not attend them; he would help her, but then he would make her pay forfeits of a sexual nature. It had died out eventually, but now that she was left alone at night, she would ring him just as she was falling asleep; he would reassure her that if anything disturbed her, he could be there in a couple of minutes. He would sleep downstairs fully dressed just in case.

Once Ramiro returned, it became essential for Mia to get away. Charlie could hardly go with her and the children as well. So, she took her mother and also went to Tenerife. Charlie was terribly lonely, and one night, he arranged to meet an old girlfriend, just for company, really. They went for a drink at the Epping Post House; looking up, he saw Ramiro glowering at him, and checking the registry book how in heaven's name he had followed him or even why, was a mystery.

Chapter 18
The Happy Hour

When Mia arrived back home, they booked into the Grove Hotel for a few hours. Mia was looking forward to showing him her new tan. Charlie gave one of his better performances; anxious as usual, he asked her if it was going to be enough, she groaned and said it was just right. He asked her if she had met anyone on holiday. She said as a matter of fact, she had, someone attached himself to her and been good company for all of them. The two of them went from strength to strength.

Charlie took her in to meet Aidan and asked him to act in both their divorces. The hatred and revenge from Ramiro continued; he had been demoted at work and could no longer expect a store for himself. Charlie slowly and carefully began to gain the children's confidence, not by hugging and kissing them, but by exploring the areas they would entirely enjoy most. Playing games with them and encouraging them in any activities that interested them. Olivia fell in love with Suzie, one of the dogs. Aidan had warned them to be careful and discreet, so they were terribly restricted in their actions, a holiday was out of the question, but they planned for when they could go to any of the wonderful places Charlie had been to already. This was the love he had been waiting for, their natures were identical; their tastes as well. Mia had started to re-stock his wardrobe and would go miles to find real bargains at D&J.

Most weekends, Charlie had to work on Saturdays, and Mia on Sunday mornings, so they took whatever they could, where they could, his car turned into Mia's office, store room and bedroom, she was excited by the risk and enjoyed most coming together in the car, usually in the forest or some dark car park, and once they were both desperate, behind some bushes in the forest in broad daylight.

She booked into the Ridgeway for a couple of nights, when things had deteriorated dangerously, taking an ensuite room with a four poster.

As Charlie was leaving at 6.30 a.m., she flashed herself out of the window as a going away treat, not realising that two guys in a parked van enjoyed just the same eyeful. Her original shyness with Charlie had turned into completely the opposite. She loved to disport her body by now, which he of course found irresistible. On a day trip to Aylesbury, they wandered up the high street; stepped into a tea shop, and searched for toys for the girls. In a joke and novelty shop, they made some small purchases, the purpose of which escaped Charlie until during this break at the Ridgeway. His cigarette exploded and he jumped out of his skin; later, his tea tasted funny. A giggling Mia told him she had put fart powder in it. Fortunately, his constitution coped with this. Or she might have got more than she bargained for.

Charlie counted his blessings every time they were together and wondered in awe how she had ever been attracted to him in the first place. During the school holidays, she would take the girls down to her parents bringing them back each weekend for Ramiro to have. She would still phone continuously.

A month after she returned from Tenerife, she had a surprise visitor at her house. Salih, the guy who had attached himself to her there turned up one day, much to Ramiro's puzzlement and Mia's embarrassment; obviously, she had not told him about her love for Charlie probably because her mother was with her. She had told him that she was getting a divorce; later, he started to write to her. She would show those letters to Charlie, and he told her she should put the poor guy in the picture. It wasn't fair to him not to know the real story. Mia said yes, she would, but she didn't see any harm in it. He was just a nice friend, so why hurt him? On her birthday she received a bunch of red roses from him, also he would phone her from time to time. He had taken a job in Qatar and was away most of the year.

Charlie was never jealous; how could he be, but he did ask Mia again to tell the truth, and put him out of his misery, as obviously he was very interested in her. One night Mia made a frightening discovery; the phone in her house was bugged. Ramiro had been listening to all her calls, how long for, what had been said, what point was there in it anyway? He had also had her post redirected, had stopped paying housekeeping, and continued to intimidate her on every occasion. Still, she stuck it out at the house, which by this time was up for sale.

She started to store all her personal possessions at Charlie's; he enjoyed having her belongings around him, and between the two of them, they now had to use every public phone for miles around. She had been having trouble with her wisdom teeth, and booked into Holy House, the local clinic, to have them extracted. Charlie spent the whole evening with her there; he had never actually seen her in a nightie before and since she kept falling out of the front of it, he got quite worked up even though they could hardly expect to take a chance in the circumstances. When he eventually left just before midnight, he got some very strange looks from the night staff.

Charlie was still involved with his Rotary work and Mia helped him to type out the lists and find new schools to write to. He was immensely proud when she put on a brief appearance at one of the rounds. He was asked to help at a charity auction in the Hawkey Hall. Mia came along with the girls as it was a public meeting, and he bought her a second-hand typewriter for Charlotte. His Rotary friends and their wives had all been shocked when he and Kat split up. Here for the first time was his 'new woman'; many of them dropped him, but several of his close friends remained.

In May, Charlie took his mother to Bath, where that year's international meeting was being held, how he wished Mia could have come with him, but of course, it was impossible. They had recorded music tapes for each other's pleasure, he had taped Phantom of the Opera for her, and she gave him Les Misérables, this last became their favourite. They played it until they knew it off by heart.

And one magic evening, they joined the queue outside the theatre where it was on, neither of them had much hope of getting in, but to their overwhelming joy, they got two front seats; it was the most wonderful evening of his life. Charlie had never felt so much emotion. The feeling between the two of them was so strong, that it could almost be seen and touched, and it would remain forever as 'their evening.' It was such a peak, that they knew it would be impossible to ever match again.

They had felt it once before on their outing to Maldon, but on that occasion, she was still with Ramiro and their parting then had broken the spell. When she had to go home to him, this time there was nothing to spoil it for them. It was a memory to cherish until they died. Mia loved the theatre, he had to see the new Jeffry Archer play, *Not a Shadow of a Doubt*, but it had been rather heavy, not exactly entertaining. They had shared choices of food; they both loved Chinese and Italian cooking. Their favourite eating places became regular haunts; often they would have a date away at Charlie's home for by now his mother had recognised that this really was going to work, and made both Mia and the children genuinely welcome. Charlie taught her to play backgammon and canasta which she loved.

Ramiro had still not accepted the facts, and now he was having them trailed by a private detective. He had also fixed devices to both their cars so that it was easy to follow them. It was as if he was acting out of the plot of his favourite spy novels. Mia had claimed that she did not enjoy cooking; the girls preferred junk food and Ramiro didn't like her meals. He would have a large lunch, fish and chips in the car on the way home and then whatever she had got ready. For Charlie, she produced some of her specials, bringing him down chicken noodle soup and apple cake. She made the most artistic birthday cakes for the girls, and she had a real talent for working with materials. She could run up anything from a dress to a full set of curtains or drapes, seemingly without effort, and of a quality and finish, better than the highest professional standards.

Slowly and carefully, Charlie rebuilt her shattered self-confidence, encouraging her to become her own woman and helping her to realise just what her true potential was after the years she had spent under the influence of Ramiro. He had considered her his intellectual and social inferior, and his family had put her down since the beginning; after all, she had trapped their son by getting pregnant and the poor fool had only married her out of common decency. She was well beneath him, and her family had no money.

They still had their lunchtime together. They had found a lovely spot in the forest of Theydon Bois where they would meet. The first time there Mia needed to have a wee, nothing unusual for her, but this was in their early days together squatting down by the back of the car. Lawrie could, of course, hear her, then glancing in his side mirror, he saw that she was actually in full view, he wanted to laugh, but he didn't know if it would embarrass her, so he sat there choking and trying unsuccessfully to look away. On one occasion, when they tried a new place that was just off the main High Road, they were amused to see a peeping tom in action; he had nothing to watch them for, but a young couple in a white Escort was really going to town, the man was on top in the front seat, really hammering away, the peeper was hopping from knee to knee.

Mia was fascinated watching them and Charlie was deflated; no way could he last as long as that himself. They had found a hotel in Barking that they used sometimes, creeping out at midnight and separating. Mia introduced him to Docklands; at one time she and Ramiro had planned to buy a townhouse there; she also discovered the Barbican Centre and took him there for the first time, where they found the London Exhibition.

When they were out together, she would hang on to his arm or they would walk with their arms around each other, oblivious to anyone else. She showed her love in so many ways, but she would seldom speak it aloud, their lovemaking had become a real pleasure; afterwards, she would explore him inquisitively, like a mother monkey, picking out small spots and squeezing any blackheads. One wet Sunday afternoon they drove to Alexander Palace which was in the process of being restored. They raced one another around almost the entire perimeter and since there was obviously some event going on, paid to go inside. Of all things, it turned out to be a Socialist party rally, celebrating the anniversary of NHS. Various bands were playing and the Labour Party's big guns were out in force, Hattersley and Kinnock walked by.

Mia spotted Glynis Kinnock; familiar faces were everywhere. They decided to wait for Kinnock's speech because it was going to be televised. In the meantime, they wandered around all the various stalls plastering each other with stickers and wearing NAL60 hats; they accidentally went into a reserved bar and sat next to an elderly lady, whom they took to be Neil Kinnock's mum, but who Charlie then recognised as Barbara Castle. Then they positioned themselves in front of the TV cameras, jumping up and down with their balloons, running home to watch the news.

On a visit to Islington, they found a second-hand record shop open, and Mia found one of Charlie's favourite old LPs by Gordon Lightfoot; she would go to great lengths to find records that he mentioned, somewhere his favourite Bob Dylan LP. She had started house hunting in Woodward; it seemed the best way to begin their future together would be for her to have her own place with the girls whilst they became accustomed to the break from their father and got used to Charlie being around.

Olivia was very possessive of her mother's attention but by now she no longer felt threatened by Charlie. He obviously saw more of her than her sister and played games with her, whenever he could. Her snowman doll had ended up in the dustbin when Ramiro saw it, but Mia rescued it and cleaned it up. Charlie found that Snakes and Ladders was a lot more frustrating than he thought; he never once beat her at it, but then she did cheat a lot. By the time she was four, she had become an accomplished dominoe player. She really did know which ones to play, and in what order, she would come out with 'My mummy is a liar' or 'mummy is a whore' not having any idea what she was saying of course. She would frequently say, 'My daddy says you must never touch me,' usually when she was sitting on his lap, or playing spiders with him. Charlotte was going to be far more difficult to get through to; she was that much older and was of course a daddy's girl.

Her father naturally played on this. He was very lonely and when he would start crying, she was drawn closer and closer to him. She unfortunately had inherited his weight problem and Charlie was well aware of the future problems this would cause her. She was no more spoilt than most of the little girls and whereas Olivia was cute and very sharp, Charlotte was quieter and much more sensitive. Charlie found her really pulling at his heartstrings, Ollie was one of the life winners she would be equally happy with anyone. Charlotte, he sensed needed kid glove handling, but if he could only get her to respond to him, he would be able to help her emotionally in so many ways. When she fell off her bike in the park one day when they were playing, her tears brought home most forcefully to him just how much he had come to feel for her. He would laugh to Mia at the prospect of having to pay for two Jewish weddings. Their eventual hope was that in a couple of years when he proved that the girls would be happy and well with him, they would move down to the country near her parents and hopefully, with Charlie's mum buy a really good hotel together.

The prospect of this future filled Charlie with excitement and anticipation to have finally this wonderful new life with this gorgeous girl who loved him so and with whom he could share every emotion and thought and to watch the girls grow up to become little replicas of their mother. It was more happiness than he ever dreamed could exist for him.

Chapter 19
Self-Destruction

After Mia's initial mention of having a child of her own, the idea became rooted in Charlie's mind, but he doubted that it would ever really happen. He had no reason to suppose that he would in fact be able to father one; it had never happened with anyone before, but he remembered the gypsy who had foretold right at the beginning with Mia, two women in your life will always love you, one much younger than the other, and you will have a son by the time you are 50.

Kat, he knew still loved him in spite of everything. Mia obviously loved him and was the other, so who knew, the prediction had been right in everything else she had said. Maybe even that might come true. After all, 50 was still two years away, a lot could happen in two years.

More often than not, they did not bother with condoms anymore; several times when Mia had been at her most fertile, they had slipped up, but apart from one of two anxieties at the time, nothing happened. Reinforcing Charlie's doubts about his potency, and then on his 48th birthday, Mia decided to give him a treat in the actual office. Locking the front door, they went into James's back office and put two chairs together to form a bridge; they had an exciting risky quickie.

Laughing together afterwards, Charlie said, "Whoops, sorry about that, darling."

Mia said more seriously, "It only takes just one little cell you know." Charlie never gave any serious consideration, why would he?

At first, she was just a bit overdue; nothing to worry about, but a week later, with still nothing. Mia carried out a do-it-yourself test and told Charlie she wasn't positive for the result. Still not really worried at all, Charlie watched with her the next Sunday in the office. Whilst she performed the test again, she told him that if the tube turned blue it would indicate positive. He had to answer a phone call whilst they were waiting and when he went into the back room again, a very white Mia was holding a very blue tube. Total disbelief was his immediate response, it couldn't, it just simply couldn't be possible, and then the unbelievable truth hit him. He felt for the first and only time, the 'oh my god,' ten feet tall bursting with love and pride and gratitude feelings, that he had never known existed. Tears raced to the back of his eyes; his heart leapt into his throat; his head swam with how he loved her.

Holding her in his arms, he said her name over and over, "Oh, Mia dear, please forgive me, how could I do this?" He cried, "I just can't credit it has happened." Shakily, they sat down together, grasping hands and staring into each other's eyes. They drove in silence into the countryside, ending up at Hatfield House, lost in their thoughts and plans; obviously, there were only two alternatives.

Normally, the historic house would have been a pleasure, but their minds were filled with confusion. They sat in the tearooms and wandered around the motor museum, Charlie floating in absolute euphoria, but torn with fear. He wanted this child so much, it would be a son he knew, but he just dared think about it. Mia was the only one who could decide, how could be otherwise, he couldn't, wouldn't and shouldn't try and influence her in any way. It must be her free choice. The problems would be huge, they listed them together; neither of them could expect to be divorced in time. Her family would think she was doing the same as she had with Ramiro. Her father would never forgive her, the girls, how would it affect them, her divorce, what would be the cost, what would she lose, where could they live, the future plans, would they be able to afford to carry them out with a new baby. Charlie's mother what would she say, and Kat, what on earth would it do to her now?

Slowly and carefully, Charlie went through the list with her; he swore to her that nothing, absolutely nothing would be unsurmountable if she agreed to have it, no matter what the problem, or how long it took, it would he promised, be sorted in time, but if she decided against it, he equally swore he would understand, and totally support her decision. Mia made her decision. First, they would get an official test carried out; if that too was positive, she felt that she would have to get an abortion. It had after all been a mistake. There was just too much against it at this time; it would cause just too much hardship and trouble.

Charlie thought his whole soul turned to ice, but somehow, he managed to keep this from showing to Mia. He pretended to agree, but inside his heart was grieving, oh, no suppose this is the gypsy's prediction, no it couldn't be it was far too soon. He begged Mia for just one thing. "Promise me, darling, that we will put it right later, it's the only way I can live with it now."

His fatherhood had lasted just one day. He phoned Aidan and told him. Then he and Mia went together to see him in his office; he explained that yes, it would complicate the divorce and possibly the settlement, but that there was nothing to stop them from having it if they wanted. He told them that he personally was against abortion, but again it had to be Mia's decision. They went to a pregnancy testing advice centre near Holborn; a most seedy-looking upstairs establishment. Mia went in alone. Charlie paced the pavement, no way was he going to let Mia use this place, no matter what it cost, she would have it done properly at a clinic. This looked and felt like an old-fashioned back street job, and for the first time, he was frightened stiff of her having the actual operation, suppose something went wrong, suppose she was damaged and couldn't have anymore. God, suppose she died, a mental picture of Charlotte formed in his mind; it stayed there ever afterwards whenever he thought about it. Suppose Ramiro hadn't married her, would little Charlotte ever have existed, wasn't that exactly what they were destroying now?

Mia came down with the news; it was positive, his particular agency had arrangements with a place in another part of London, and obviously, they would have to go somewhere more local. Mia got down to some serious planning. She arranged the place and time; she confided in her friend Sue, who agreed to have both the girls for the day, and she arranged to go on holiday with her mother and the children immediately afterwards. All Charlie had to do was to provide the money and somehow live with his feelings.

He discussed his fears for her safety with her, but she minimised them; "It's nothing serious these days," she said, "if I go in at 10, I'll be out by 1.30." On the actual morning, Charlie felt so ill and frightened for her, and so much in love that he could barely go through the motions at work, rooted by the phone, waiting and waiting. Mia rang him and said all was ok. The next day she told him there were no apparent after-effects, but she had been warned that sometimes it could change one's sexual feelings; obviously, this couldn't happen to them though.

Chapter 20
The First Cracks

Charlie was left alone once more, worried for her that something would go wrong in Spain, empty inside for the disappointment he felt, miserable to be left behind again and loving her every moment, trying to understand her decision and convincing himself that she had been right. He took a few days off and went to Scotland again looking up an old girlfriend in Troon. She had been deserted by her husband, and years before Charlie had a brief affair with her. She was nice to see again, they had an enjoyable, 'do you remember evening,' but just couldn't get Mia out of his mind for a moment and he longed for her return.

She sent him a letter explaining her feelings and reassuring him. And came the day of her return; she rushed down to his hotel. Charlie persuaded her some time before that with her figure and looks, she could easily wear the more fashionable casual clothes that her younger sisters wore. Dubiously at first and then wholeheartedly, Mia had started wearing miniskirts, and there she was at his door, beautifully tanned with a tiny black skirt and a striking black top with a gold motif pattern. She literally took his breath away; she was home.

That weekend at the beginning of September was the very first time they had been able to stay together. The girls had gone away with Ramiro, and the two of them had their longest and best time together. Mia had made Charlie promise never to bring up the subject of abortion again. She said that she needed to put it at the back of her mind, so she could pretend it hadn't happened. It had been a crucial time for them, but they were over it. Certainly, their lovemaking had not suffered for by the time Mia got back from Spain, her urges were at their peak. They had not been active for over a month, but they certainly made up for it now.

Mia had made two decisions whilst she was away; the first was that instead of buying a house in Woodward, she would in fact buy one near her parents. Charlie agreed that until they were ready for the future, he would keep his existing hotel going unless something really good came up first down Mia's way. He also agreed with Kat that she would receive her property settlement from him prior to any divorce, which meant he would finance and borrow the money.

Mia's second decision was that she would be fitted with a contraceptive device so as not to have to trust anything else or take any risks again; this she duly did, and after about a month's discomforts, settled down to it. Charlie had to admit it was better for him than wearing condoms but equally, he found that he didn't really like the new feeling much. He had actually enjoyed Mia's professionalism with condoms. She would cheekily tear the packet open with her teeth and spit the end out, then fix them on him behind her back, without even looking. Her expertise at this always made him grin, and in a way, he missed that, this new style seemed a bit clinical, and sometimes he thought he could actually feel it.

Her divorce was proceeding slowly before it all blew up—Ramiro the great property speculator—had bought a new flat in Stamford Hill, that when it was finished would show a nice profit. Mia had taken Charlie to see it one day on the pretext of giving a free valuation. It was in fact a very good buy or would have been, but the deal went wrong, and Ramiro had to borrow from his father to complete it. Now in order to sell it, he had to get Mia to sign the release papers, and she would not agree unless he equally agreed to her own final settlement; the hatred and the anger flowed even more, and the pressures built up to boiling point again.

Kat, by this time, was also pressing for settlement; they had been parted for a year, and she was still hurting all the time. Charlie would go and visit her once a month, to pay her £100 per week, which he had been giving her all along, and although these visits were painful for both of them, they seemed to help her slowly come to terms. Each time he felt she would cling to him, and he could feel the emotion in her. But Mia filled his every desire and he was unable to respond to her other than in kindness. He didn't feel guilty, just very sad for Kat, and he would try to make things better for her as much as he could; consequently, when the settlement figure between them had been worked out, he gave her voluntarily as much more as he could afford to borrow, in extra £10000 in fact not to be generous, not because it eased his guilt.

Simply, it was Kat, and he wanted her to be as comfortable as possible. He told Mia that he was going to do this now and that it would cast them some £900 per month which meant that apart from his deals, he would be quite hard up for a while. She replied that she quite understood that perhaps they wouldn't be able to go out as often as before, but she was happy just to come to his home now. She asked him if he was certain that this was what he wanted to do, and he said yes, of course, he had to pay Kat anyway, the sooner, the better.

Chapter 21
Carry on Loving

Mia had been advised that she should keep a diary of events with Ramiro. He was still tapping the phone and threatening to release the dirty video he had of her. She decided to play him at his own game and tried to go at him into making his verbal threats again whilst she had a mini tape recorder hidden under her jumper. She did in part succeed in this, but as she walked away from him, the red record light shone through the back of her clothes and he forcibly took it from her. One night, she snatched his car keys and drove off to search the vehicle. He did this to hers all the time as well as taking her handbag and ransacking her room. He immediately reported to the police that she had stolen it. He eventually agreed to hand over the video if he would sign the papers for the flat.

Aidan advised her not to, but she did it anyway. Ramiro swore on children's lives that there were no other copies, but Mia found one in his car. She edited out all the actual film leaving him with a blank tape, and she destroyed the original he had returned to her. She rang Charlie at the office to say she was watching it first, and when he suggested he would like to see it, she laughed and said no she thought perhaps it was a bit too revealing so she burnt it.

They attended Bridget's wedding earlier in the year, Mia had bought a new outfit for the occasion, a most attractive pale khaki jumpsuit. It looked most complicated to wear with pockets and buttons and zips anywhere, but in fact, she could slip out of it in literally seconds, which she demonstrated on more than one occasion. Bridget had fallen pregnant within a month of getting married, which was exactly as predicted, but the sadness for Charlie was that it was just about the same time as Mia and he had to put up with all the attention Bridget received and watch her pregnancy develop. Knowing all the time that Mia would have been exactly the same, it hurt him every day to look at her. But of course, he had to keep it to himself.

Before the summer ended, the two of them went 'Royal chasing' on the spur of the moment. A cousin of the Queen was getting married in Saffran Walden and Mia directed them to the Baronial Hall where it was taking place. They missed seeing the Royal party by a couple of minutes only, but it was great fun ogling at the other guests. They still did a lot of simple things together that gave them great pleasure. Having tea in a quiet little tea shop in Waltham Abbey, and then wandering around the market, shopping together in every high street store in the district and in Oxford Street. He would spend hours trying to find the type of historical video films that he knew she would enjoy. Anne of Thousand Days, The Lion in the Winter, Les Misérables; he loved to watch her pleasure when she saw what they were, just like a little girl herself sometimes.

Both her sister Harper and her sister Shirley now had regular boyfriends. Shirley particularly had Ian, who Charlie liked immensely, they would often come to the hotel with Mia, and Charlie thoroughly enjoyed their company at first. He had been concerned by the age difference, but they all shared the same tastes and shared same things, and a perfectly natural friendship developed. Mia would never phone him from her parents' home, always going out to use a phone box, and as the months passed, Charlie began to wish that he could get to know her parents. Mia's father was only five years older than Charlie and she was afraid that it would be difficult and embarrassing. Charlie understood her feelings on this but being cut out of a whole area of her life hurt him constantly. Just before the winter set in, a hotel in East Uckfield came on the market.

Charlie took Mia and his mother to see it and it would have been ideal if only the timing had been right. He was hopeful that it would give Mia encouragement for their future; it was just the type of hotel he dreamed of; the girls would have a lovely life there, of the style Ramiro could never compete against, and he could see how this would benefit Charlotte. This would be the life that she would be most happy in and would prefer to return to, rather than stay with him. Mia however seemed still to prefer her own plan to start with and since he had not sold his own place anyway, it was only an outside possibility, but it did prove that the right sort of place was going to be a reality, not just a dream.

They fulfilled one of their promised pleasures originally. They had planned a weekend in a special hotel in Oxford; they couldn't manage that, but they did go for one day, wandering around the colleges, and having tea in the upstairs tea rooms full of students, soaking up the history and atmosphere, and promising themselves that they would do it properly on day. They would still sometimes make love in his car, and one dark night when they were in the forest, using the front passenger seat, Mia was on top wearing only Charlie's black jacket and looking extremely sexy, Charlie was aware that he was failing her, it was exciting, it should have been successful, but he just could not match her needs, and he didn't know why.

On the night of the Jarre Docklands open-air concert, Charlie arranged to pick Mia up at Victoria Station. As he drove up through the east end, he was listening to the live broadcaster on the radio and at the same time he could see the laser beams and fireworks; driving back with her, they became enthralled with it and determined to get in if they could. They managed to get within one building of the actual show, just in time for the finale, but they heard it live and felt the excitement of it. Harper and Eric, her boyfriend, were actually there, but Charlie and Mia were home in half an hour. Harper was stuck until 5 a.m. and had passed out in the crowd, and missed most of the concert anyway. Charlie felt that being old and experienced did have some advantages after all.

Mia was existing on her overdraft; Ramiro had paid no housekeeping at all and consequently, she was usually hard up. Charlie wanted to treat her to some nice clothes and he persuaded her to let him take her to the west end. He loved watching her try on the various styles, and she settled on two very attractive outfits. His favourite was a lovely pale pink dress with a scalloped cross-over front; she wore this for the office Christmas party coming up, especially from her parents on the train. Charlie was immediately proud of her because this year, they really were together as a pair; they didn't have to pretend to anyone, but strangely she didn't seem to be really enjoying herself much. He felt that she had only come so as not to disappoint him, rather than because she wanted to.

He had cheated like hell this year because there were worthwhile cash bonuses, depending on the office position. He didn't actually win, because the losers would have demanded an investigation, but he was determined to be second. He very nearly miscalculated which would have been awful trouble, and was vastly relieved about the result. The party was once again at the Princess Consort. Charlie had taken Mia there for her birthday dinner, and that night, they had booked into the hotel part for the evening. This time however they went back to his own hotel making love happily, and then having a pre-Christmas drink with Charlie's mum and Aunt Betty. Once again, he drove her down to Haywards Heath. She sat with her feet up on the dashboard and they laughed and talked fondly as the miles sped by. He hoped and hoped that she would suggest that this year he should come in and meet her parents; it was Christmas, what better time? What a lovely present that would be for him, but once again they parked around the corner and again, he drove all the way home alone.

Chapter 22
The Christmas Spirit

As it seemed most likely that this would be the last Christmas in his hotel, Charlie had decided that his mother deserved one final family Christmas with as much of the family as possible. As far as he personally was concerned, his own festivities would not start until Mia arrived on Boxing Day. But he was more than happy to have the place filled with uncles, aunts, cousins and nephews. His cousin Sandra, the lovely young blond of years ago arrived with her two sons, her second husband and her parents.

They had taken the invitation to be for a full week, rather than just the four days anticipated, and Sandra had changed out of all proportions from being a slim and sexy young woman. There she had not had the best of luck; her first husband had run off with her best friend and she had struggled to bring her young sons up by herself and true fits had spoilt both the boys. And she had a terrible time with them; the youngest was a mummy's boy, who she smothered. The eldest one was much more like his father and resented not being allowed to live with him. This situation in his own family was one of the main lessons

Charlie had used in working out how to manage Mia's girls; the parallels were all there to be seen.

Sandra had been in her late 20s when her marriage broke up; she had been on her own for ten years and had become very bitter. Finally, she had remarried a man older than herself, who she bullied unmercifully and instead of turning to drink, which some girls do, she had turned to eat; she had become a female Ramiro and her vast bulk had given her an equally inflated idea of her own importance. She and Charlie clashed within hours of being together and as the holiday progressed, she got worse and worse. He just would not be intimidated by her, but equally, he was determined not to spoil his mother's big Christmas.

Mia rang him every day as usual, and he filled the hours, as best he could. But all the time he was thinking that this would be his last Christmas alone; next year, he would have the girls to pamper. He could take them to pantomime, the circus. All the things Mia had done on her own with them this year. Next year, they would have their first big holiday together in Singapore, the Far East, maybe the Caribbean, or Disneyland if they took the girls; next year, they would have everything.

His cousin Phyllida came on her own, as she did most Christmases. Her daughter always went to her father and her boyfriend went to his own children. She also had been on her own now for some ten years. Her husband David was Charlie's cousin. Phyllida was no relation at all other than by marriage, but she was thought of still as family. Charlie was very fond of her and had been best man at their wedding whilst Tracey was matron of honour. But after five or six years, Phyllida had started having a series of affairs, David had looks and money, but sexually they were poles apart. And that part of their marriage had become impossible for Phyllida. She was sensitive and sensual; David was rough and ready, he had forgiven her the first couple of times and tried his way to save the marriage, but Phyllida was determined to lead her own life again. Determined that is until David decided to get remarried.

Then she tried everything she knew to get him back and spent all the years in between regretting her decision. Their daughter had not been spoilt or harmed by the breakup. And again, Charlie used that as a lesson for the girls; he had seen so many breakups over the years, but those in his own family, together with his own early life gave him the knowledge and experience, he would need now for Mia's children. And in the previous year, he had slowly seen it working, so that by now the girls were always happy to see him.

On Christmas Eve, Charlie had received a real bonus a deal he had arranged three years previously and for which he had never been paid, rang out of the blue, come round and paid him £1500 cash. He was still owed £5000 for another deal he had done, and earlier in the year another £3000 had paid up. He had opened a joint account so that Mia knew she had some emergency security if she needed it, but they hardly touched it. All in all, money was no problem except for the loan he had taken out to pay Kat with. The previous Christmas he had worried about Kat a lot, thinking how miserable it was for her she had spent it with her own children and family, but he knew full well how much it hurt her. Now this year, she had her own new home; he hadn't heard from her for three months and he was relieved that she was getting on with her own life at last.

Mia arrived having handed the girls over to Ramiro. She illuminated the whole party just by being there and for Charlie, Christmas finally began. She was rather quiet in the presence of all these new members of the family, but once her shyness wore off, she was a real delight, acting out charades and egging Charlie on. His mother and Auntie Betty were delighted to have her, both of them were really fond of her by now and she soon felt completely at home. Charlie took her up to his bedroom to give her his main surprise present he had of course bought her several other little personal gifts that he had loved getting for her. But his big surprise she had no idea of. He had spent his entire office bonus on a combined stereo tape deck, radio and CD player. And he had set it all up ready for her. Now he made her close her eyes, lie on the bed and wait whilst he switched it onto one of her favourite tracks of the moment a release of the Hollies 'He Ain't Heavy.'

The real pleasure and astonishment in her eyes gave him more pleasure himself than he could ever remember. He told her it was for her new home, and he said again, that she was not to worry he would see that when she did get her own place, she would want for nothing in it; he would see to that. Again, he thought how much he wanted to marry her, but obviously, she wasn't ready for this. Her divorce couldn't be that far off now, maybe they could just get engaged, that would make him feel so much better about it, just as long as she was still happy. That night when they went to bed, they made love gently to each other at first, then more and more passionately. Mia was loving and affectionate and they revelled in each other in all their favourable ways, listening and enjoying her new present until the small hours.

Sleeping the whole night together was still something of a rarity for them. Charlie still would only doze. He loved just lying there watching her sleep and waking to see her still there was a supreme pleasure. For New Year's Eve, Mia cooked her first goose, Charlie's traditional once-a-year favourite, she did a superb job of the whole thing; for someone who had professed not to enjoy cooking, she certainly had taken to it for him. It was like everything that Mia turned her hand to, if it interested her, she had the very highest standard. For Charlotte, she had traded a garden slide for a special Cindy doll house. She and Charlie had spent an evening making furniture for it, as the actual ready-made furniture was very expensive. Charlie was good at model making, but Mia did nearly all the work. And her finished items were better than the bought ones. For his mother, she made some cushion covers with applique flowers on; they were absolutely beautiful and gave his mother more pleasure than anything that could have been bought for her. She proudly showed them to anyone and everyone as 'Look what Mia made for me.'

Chapter 23
The Ides of March

She developed a passion for lime soaking, and they went everywhere looking at old oak furniture. She spent hours stripping an old card table she had. Ramiro then smashed it up and threw it out; she showed him an expensive dresser in an exclusive local shop and he determined to buy it for her, but it was too early, he would wait until later and surprise her. At this period, after the traumas of the previous summer, their love seemed to be at an even greater peak than it had been at the beginning.

Ramiro had repossessed her trusty red 'oldie' and Mia's father obtained a new car for her. He bought it from a local priest, and whilst Mia appreciated it greatly, it was not at all the car she would have chosen for herself. She determined to pay him for it from her eventual settlement, but unfortunately, it didn't last long enough. It actually didn't last more than a couple of weeks; it may have been blessed. On her way back from her parents, it broke down at the entrance to the Dartford tunnel. Charlie went flying down the motorway to pick her and the girls up, took them home and then he and Mia spent four hours waiting for the AA to show up. They failed, down it went, towed to her parents, up it came again, broke down again, and once more down again; this time it stayed, and eventually oldie returned, freshly sprayed.

Ramiro was obviously up to something. The divorce was set for March; there was a buyer for their house and it seemed finally Mia's ordeal would be over, but by mid-February, a change seemed to have come over her that Charlie perceived but couldn't understand. Her affection towards him no longer seemed to come naturally; she seemed to be concentrating far more on what appeared to be her plans for the future, rather than their eventual plans. She hurt him repeatedly by her attitude, their lovemaking became intermittent and she found excuses not to stay with him rather than looking for ways that they could be together.

One night, they went to a charity performance of Billy Connolly, whose rudeness was a joint favourite of theirs; they enjoyed the same authors as well, and Tom Sharpe had become a favourite, discovering wilt together they would share all the main characters and ludicrous plots. Mia's sense of humour was identical to Charlie's, he liked to discover and use strange words in everyday conversation. Mia picked up on this and came out with some beauties of her own. Showing off his knowledge of geography, Charlie had asked her to name a country beginning, but not ending with A, very hard if you don't know the answer first. They then went onto what's the capital of, with Charlie again showing off; finally, Mia opened the AA book and said, "How are you on reservoirs?" shutting him up and shooting him down simultaneously.

She had that some quickness in her mind as his own, and they would bounce things back and forward between themselves. He could never think of a single moment when they had been bored with each other's company. She enjoyed all his stories; he loved listening to the sound of her voice. When they dined out in a restaurant, he would point out to her the obviously married couples, each sitting there with nothing left to say to each other. They both realised the value of mutual interest; it was a rarity between the couples. But obviously, it was one of the special things that they had for each other; it never failed. Mia's aloofness did cause a failure though.

Charlie worried and fretted as to what was wrong, and one rainy day, when she had met him at an appointment, he had in a block of flats in Forest Court. He phoned her to just sit in his car and listen to him. He explained gently that he could not go on being hurt and warned her that they were in danger of ruining their relationship if she went this way. He suggested that they needed a break before any permanent damage was done. What on earth was it that was wrong anyway?

She cried; told him she knew she had been hurting him. She couldn't explain what was wrong but promised to be more consistent. 'No,' she didn't want a break; they clung to each other and he could literally feel the relief flow over him, saying they should have a break was one thing but actually doing it would have been impossible for him and yet he hadn't been bluffing. Things had somehow started to come apart between them. It had become a one-way love. The cruellest of all now, it was one in the open and thank god, she was her old self again. He thought it might have been in fear of the court case looming over her, or the accumulation of such a long period of strain in spite of all his efforts on her behalf, some of it, even a lot of it must have left an effect.

Shortly after, the divorce did in fact go through, after umpteen meetings with Aidan and his assistant Hughes, and after meetings with Mia's lady barrister, and after delays and alterations, finally, it happened. The settlement was thrashed out there and then. The sale of the house had been hanging on by the skin of its teeth. Ramiro had been threatening reprisals, swearing to Mia that he would hate her forever as only Jews knew how, an eye for an eye, etc., promising her that as soon as the girls were old enough, he would give them all the evidence of her lies and deceit.

On the day of the hearing, he turned up with a whole gaggle of his lawyers, including a senior partner. Mia bravely saw it through. Charlie had always told her that in a confrontation in court between her and Ramiro, there could only be one result, especially if he lost control of himself. He had become a totally unsympathetic figure, weak and spiteful, not much of a man at all. He deserved all he got for his actions since the beginning, and it was his own selfishness and abuse of her which caused her to lose her love for him in the first place. Charlie would have preferred Mia not to have taken quite so much off him, but it was her choice, not his. He knew he would make sure the girls were not turned against their father.

Ramiro should be grateful it was only him that Mia had fallen for; it could have been much worse if it had been someone greedy. Both of them were sworn over to keep certain rooms in the house until the sale was completed and the figure for Mia was based on the agreed sale price. Unfortunately, the sale fell off the next day. Things had improved though; he was now her ex-husband. Mia could come and go to suit herself and she could bring the girls to Charlie's in complete safety at last.

They achieved another of their little dreams, going for a day trip to Calais. Mia had never been to France before and they had long intended to go. Setting off early, they arrived at Dover just after 8 a.m., had a nice easy ferry ride over, and then walked into the old town. Charlie took them in the wrong direction and as they walked all the way back, they were apprehended by the customs men and questioned at some length. Arm in arm, happy and relaxed, they crossed the railway line and strolled past the huge old Townhall, window shopping in the high street and enjoying all the atmosphere they had a typical long French lunch and Charlie found it highly amusing when Mia came back from the 'Ladies' in acute embarrassment. She got her own back when he had to go. He hadn't realised just how open it really was. They just missed a ferry and had to hang about for the next one. But it had been a trip that fulfilled all their expectations.

In the duty-free shop, Charlie on impulse bought a bottle of Bushmills Irish whisky; he never touched whisky himself, but he had the idea that maybe he could save it for when he met Mia's father. She would now come down to his hotel most evenings depending on what time Ramiro came home. He had started staying away for two or three nights at a time, on business he claimed. This meant Mia had to get used to being in the house alone at night. And gradually, she conquered her fears. Towards the end of March, a bombshell descended on Charlie at work. He was told that he was being 'promoted' to the main Barkingside office; he had no choice in the matter at all, and it was the last thing he wanted. But he decided that finances being what they were, he would at least give it a try.

The whole thing felt very suspicious to him. He definitely smelt a rat. He had won the sales competition in February and so it was arranged for them to all go out for dinner once more. They chose, of course, to go to their favourite restaurant in Chingford, where it had all started with Mia. Bridget was leaving at the end of the month to have her baby, and Charlie sadly broke the news to all of them that this would be their goodbye; the last supper as a group; it was a shame, but he had Mia's love and that made everything else bearable.

Chapter 24
Storm Warning

He had a couple of weeks of leave saved up and he took them at the start of April. Now that Ramiro could no longer legally object, they took the girls out together for a day at Windsor Safari Park. The girls were both happy and excited and had no trouble at all. Charlie had a love of zoos himself and so it was a pleasure for him to go to this one. The kids loved going anywhere in his car. They would play with the electric windows and sunroof to their heart's content, whilst they were driving slowly through the lion's enclosure, Charlie was forcibly reminded just how careful you have to be with children taking you literally. He pointed out a lion that was trolling past roaring and said to Olivia, " Can you hear that roar?"

"No," she said, pressing her window control down so that she would be able to. Total panic ensured for a couple of seconds. The sea world display with whales and dolphins was a special highlight. Charlie planned to have lots more treats like this in the summer for them, thinking carefully just what little girls would like most fun fairs, of course, the seaside, a farm. He knew that there was a special children's section where they could pick up lambs and piglets, ponies etc. He and Mia were careful not to be too close in front of the girls of course, but the fun of all being together more than made up for it. Mia had taken the girl's pony riding at High Beech, with her twin sisters.

Olivia had been too young to try, and Charlotte unfortunately was frightened when her pony ran away. So, it wasn't very successful. Later, Mia and Charlie took Olivia for a walk in the same part of the forest; he wished he had thought to bring his dogs along and planned to do so next time. Aidan owed him some money and invited the two of them out to dinner. This was the very first invitation they had ever had as a couple, most of their original friends had joint ones with their former partners, and they decided to go to Ho Ho's, a very expensive Chinese restaurant. Mia wore Charlie's favourite jumpsuit; she looked fabulous as usual, she had only met Aidan's wife Victoria briefly before, but they soon got on well together.

Charlie was driving so he took it easy on the drink, but Aidan plied them with Saki which Mia having not tried before failed to realise the potency of, and as the meal wore on, she had more and more to drink. She certainly wasn't drunk, but she was extremely frisky, and after coffee and liqueurs when it was very late indeed, she took Charlie completely by surprise, telling him she was randy as hell. Now they could easily have gone back to his place; he would have loved her to stay the night, but she didn't want to do that. What she wanted was for them to go down the road to their old favourite dark car park. Within seconds, she was completely naked; he was astonished at just how quickly she could get out of that particular outfit once again. She was very very active, demanding really in a nice way. Charlie failed to satisfy her or even come close. She was left frustrated and disappointed; he was too, of course, but he put it down to the meal, the late hour, the place. He was aware that lovemaking had absolutely nothing to do with it, at all; this had been for Mia's needs; he had blown it.

The following week was Victoria's birthday. Charlie got hold of some Diana Ross tickets for Wembley, and the four of them went together; standing up and dancing to her fast numbers was glamorous, and very good. On the way back, they stopped and had an Italian meal in Golders Green. Of all places, Charlie was in fact off to Italy himself the very next day; he was only going because his old friend Jeremy was to be honoured. He knew that no matter how good the trip was, it would be nothing without Mia. At Lake Garda, he met up with his friends. He loved the little town of Sirmiore, wandering around the cobbled streets and squares; he must bring her back here soon. She would love it too; he stood on the balcony reputed to have been used by Romeo and Juliet.

The others were going on to Venice, one of the most romantic cities in the world; knowing it was wasted without her, he and Jeremy came home together. Having to wait four hours before their flight, Charlie was desperate to get back to Mia. Why on earth had he gone in the first place? It had only been three days, but as usual, nothing had changed. He still missed her every moment they were parted, just as much as at the beginning, he felt that this would be in a way his farewell to Rotary. He had met all his foreign friends one last time. He had supported old Jeremy with his new life and family; there would be no room or time for it anymore. He chased around the airport trying to track down an earlier flight, not easy in Italian; eventually, with less than ten minutes to spare, he got them rerouted immediately to Gatwick. Rather than wait for Heathrow to arrive back, he immediately phoned home, to be told by his mum, that Mia had just left to pick him up at Heathrow as a surprise; for the first time, their knack of almost telepathy had failed.

They had another really special weekend together driving off on a Saturday morning heading vaguely towards Oxford. They stopped first at Hampton Court; it was so lovely just to be away together that they didn't care where they actually went. The palace was a bit of a disappointment, but the gardens were lovely; they had a drink sitting out in the sunshine and then headed off again. On impulse, Mia suggested they stop at Windsor. She had been there with Ramiro and the girls, but for Charlie, it was for the first time.

They stopped at Eton, drove past the college and found a giant old hotel; the coach yard had been converted into little chalets, with a huge multi-paned bow window at the front. Walking slowly through the town, window shopping, just sauntering along together, they found an antique shop, that had some interesting old model soldiers; Charlie's long-time favourite hobby; Mia tried to persuade him to buy them for himself. But he was happy just to look. They climbed up the castle, down the Victorian display at the station and hand in hand, down by the river. Choosing where to eat for this special night together. They selected a lovely but very expensive restaurant on the bridge itself, ordering a Chateau Briand for two. They ate a leisurely and excellent meal, watching the river flow past and talking together. Charlie felt completely happy and contented.

After all the fears, frights and impossible odds, they had made it. He had no doubts. He loved her. Now even more than he had at the start. Then it had been frantic. Now it was warm and natural. This would be just one of many weekends they would enjoy.

Ramiro would get the kids. They would have each other; he wanted to go straight back to bed and make love to her. But she decided she wanted a little stroll first. Her little stroll turned into a marathon walk right up to the gates of the castle. Uphill all the way. Charlie was tired out. But couldn't admit to it in case she thought, it was his age. When they did in fact make love, it was only once. But it was just as lovely as ever. He held her in his arms all night. Feeling her breath up against his chest. Listening to her quiet little snore. Dozing and waking just to look at her again. Breakfast took an age to serve. So, they had to run all the way back to the castle. They wanted to see the changing of the guards. It turned out to be the Scots guards this time. The most exciting of all with the pipes and drums. The queen and Royal family were in residence and they strained to see through the upper windows. What they caught a glimpse of might have been Princess Anne or her car at least.

The palace itself was no disappointment; much better than Hampton Court. On the walls were displayed all the old battle flags of the old disbanded Irish regiments. Mia had once brought her grandfather's old first-war medals to Charlie. He had shown her how to identify the name, rank and regiment written around the rim. And now he showed her the actual flag that her grandfather must have seen for himself seventy years before. On the way back, they stopped at Runnymede, and he bought her a scroll showing the history of the Kings and Queens; both of them were real royalists, and they often tested each other's knowledge just for him. On the journey back, Mia seemed rather quiet and withdrawn. Charlie thought she was probably missing the girls.

Her parents had given her some money for Christmas, and she had found a place in the east end that sold leather coats at a reasonable price, just off Sidney Street. It was typical of Mia that she would have gone to so much trouble before spending the money; she really could find out the bargains; she said it was the warmest coat she had worn for years. From there, they went to the Tower of London, queuing with the tourists and school kids to see the crown jewels.

Mia founds it difficult to tear herself away from the crown; they were so absorbed that they ran out of time. And had to tear back to Woodward like loonies.

Chapter 25
The Final Countdown

His new job started badly. After the quiet little Woodward Office this was, to say the least hectic, where he had been taking on six or seven properties a week, he was now doing thirty, none of which he was sure of the price for or even where they were the staff turned out to be two boys probably the most unpleasant in the whole company and the pressure from above was incessant. He was forbidden to change anything or rock the boat, gone were the days of personal service. This was an unacceptable new face estate agency with a vengeance, and he hated it; still, he had to try, so he buried himself in work, trying to get at least some sales together on the deadest market ever.

He could not get home to help his mother with the hotel as usual so Mia did everything for them.

She would call every day, either take his mum out to the shops or do the shopping for her, collect the laundry, pick her up from the hospital, where she was having treatment, even take the dogs out walking in the park. Charlie could not have managed without her at this time and she and his mother became really close. His mother told him that she had never felt such special affection for anyone he had ever been involved with and that she could now well understand how he had fallen so completely for her.

Once the two of them went off together all day somewhere secret neither would reveal to him. Both his mother and his aunt had arranged to go away for a short holiday in May; this tied in with Ramiro having the girls and Mia moved into the hotel for four magical days. Running the place during the day, cooking the evening meals for the two of them, doing his washing and ironing, and all the other things for him, he felt that this was their peak, as good as being married in fact; the only thing missing was the girls. Every evening, he would literally rush home to her, and there she would be. At first, they used his mother's downstairs bedroom, to be on hand if there were any calls at night, using her ensuite bathroom to the full, bathing together and luxuriating; they had never managed to have so many hours with each other before, and they filled them all.

Mia had suggested that they have their first-ever dinner party on Saturday night; he invited Aidan and Victoria; she invited her sister Shirley and Ian; it was one of the first really summery nights of the year, and they decided to make it into a barbeque instead. Mia had spent hours shopping for all the right bits and preparing them. Charlie was so proud of the way she handled the whole thing; she was the perfect hostess, and it was a lovely evening in every respect but one, they got to bed very late that night, having moved to his own room, so that Shirley and Ray could stay.

Tired and happy, Charlie lay on the bed in his shorts watching Mia shower and get ready for bed, the sight of her body still thrilled him as much as ever. They had both had a lot to drink and feeling romantic and contended, he was looking forward to yet another lovemaking session where he could show her his thanks properly. Instead, she simply walked across to him and said, "Get them off," and promptly jumped on him. At first, he thought she was just joking and that they would soon settle down; instead, she became more and more aggressive. He had never seen her so desperate before; she was literally driving them faster and faster. He was left far behind her and she had barely started but she just would not stop; groaning in frustration, she ran naked out onto his private roof, he followed of course to find her bending over the parapet and offering herself in her most provocative pose; one which he usually loved, but here on the roof at 2 a.m.; it was cold and most uncomfortable. Taking her back to bed, he attempted another effort, but it was too soon for Mia and he had to resort to giving her an oral orgasm, thinking about it whilst she slept.

He tried to work out what this desperation of hers was all about, running through his mind every reason he could think of; basically, neither of them had been any good for the other, his was the failure of course, but what had brought her to this new condition. As a direct result of this weekend, Aidan invited them to come to his new place in Spain for a long weekend in June. He owed Charlie quite a bit of money for various deals; one of which they had agreed would cover any costs for both divorces, and so he offered to treat them both for nothing. Mia spent an entire morning excitedly phoning around trying to get air tickets; she was absolutely delighted with the prospect as was Charlie of course. This might not be the big special holiday they had been waiting for, but it was free, and it was soon, what could be nicer?

She upset Charlie by talking about a possible guest house she had received details of in Haywards Heath, exploring the possibility of buying it with her brother, and saying if he weren't quick, she would get on before he did. He asked her casually just in conversation really if she had heard anything further from Keith, she replied, "You don't want to know," which he found strange from her tone. She had said some months before that he wanted her to have dinner with him next time he came back, Charlie said of course it was her own business to do whatever she wanted, but that he felt that for her to give up one of their own rare evenings together would be rather unfair.

She had also mentioned that in August when Ramiro had the children, she thought she would like to go over to Ireland on her own, to look up some of her cousins. Charlie's backup plan if the two of them couldn't get away for their big holiday was to take the girls to Disneyland, so he found it strange for Mia to be thinking of using what also should have been their time. She talked also of a possible skiing holiday, which didn't excite Charlie much, but he thought that if that was what she wanted, that was what they would do. She asked him if he would babysit the girls whilst she went to work one day. Ramiro was away and she could not get anyone else; he loved the idea; both the girls were happy to stay with 'Charlie Marlie & Auntie Dora Pora.' He kept them both amused and thoroughly enjoyed himself in the process, thinking this was the way it should be now, obviously Mia trusted leaving them to him. And equally obviously the girls were content with the arrangement as well.

What a change from the days when Charlotte, filled with poison by her father, had refused to travel in Charlie's car to Victoria. And had not in fact wanted to leave him and go down to her grandparents that time, to teach her a lesson, they had all gone on the underground, much to Harper's indignation. At that time, Charlie had thought briefly that Charlotte in fact may be better off with her father. He was never going to succeed in breaking through her barriers and now here she was with him perfectly happy at last. Ollie was irresistible to everyone.

Charlotte needed much more attention, and her father compared her unfavourably with his sister's daughter. Charlie could see that she was bright enough though, perhaps slow in some areas; he was amazed when she trotted out something about static electricity, for example, he could understand that she hated school sports day, coming last in races was no fun for anyone, he thought how later on he would find sports for her that her weight would be an advantage in, javelin throwing came to mind, don't push the child into things she was bound to fail at, encourage her to develop naturally that would be the way.

Mia and he had seen a doll house kit that he wanted to get for her later, maybe she would have her mother's skills and they could build it together. When he had first known little Ollie, she had needed to stop for a wee, all the time, now she was much too grown-up for this, she was advanced for her age, writing her name clearly, counting up to ten and pretending to be able to read, she was so cute now. He just wanted to pick her up and hug all the time, but he had deliberately forced himself not to ever become demonstrative to either of them and that was how he succeeded so well.

They were never under any pressure from him; he made no demands on their emotions which would confuse them, and he never let them see that he was between them and their mother's love. Once they were away from their father's day-to-day influence, there would be plenty of time to show them physical affection, until then he would refrain himself and wait. Ollie inherited Charlotte's old bicycle; she had a way of riding it that had to be seen to believe, pedalling faster than even Mia could run. She would fly around the park, whilst never looking at where she was going. How she kept from accidents he never knew. He would look at Mia and wonder if she had been the same when she was a little girl. Just how much of their father could there be in them, they would have to wait and see, but he could foresee that the Jewish blood in Charlotte would indeed have a pull on her, her father's family, her cousins, the presents and the whole feeling of being Jewish would be very difficult for Mia and him to combat, that plus her natural feelings for her father would need very careful handling, but fortunately Charlie had years of knowing and dealing with Jewish families, probably more than even Mia herself in some respects.

Between the two of them, they would manage her. But the initial transition would be the hardest. That would be with the most damage would occur unless they were very careful. Charlie had received tickets for the Robin Day TV show and Edwina Currie was the main guest. And he arranged to take a group of the winning youngsters from his own youth speech competition, thinking how much Mia would enjoy this. He was disappointed and dismayed when she declined. He went on his own, but with no one other than the youngsters to share with; it was an anti-climax, when he got home that night there was Mia and his mother gleefully playing back the video recording and sure enough there, he was large as life, he wondered if perhaps she had been afraid of being recognised herself, but afraid of whom?

Things at work had gone from bad to worse for Charlie, the atmosphere was very intimidating; he was being ordered about like a junior, and had no authority at all.

Mia and Harper popped in one Saturday morning, and he introduced them as the bone sisters. Harper if she lost any more weight, would look like a skeleton, and Mia never seemed able to put on any weight, no matter what she ate. The yuppies were suitably impressed, the two sisters together were a lovely sight to behold, and no one could believe Mia was 28 with two children. She really did look more like a teenager herself with the style of dress she now adopted. On the Saturday before his previous birthday, Charlie had been part of a company demonstration in Valentine's Park. Harper had brought the girls over to see the carnival and fete, and she gave him a present from her and Olivia, a pot plant that grew and grew out of all proportion. He had known her of course right back from the beginning and probably because she was the sister of the girl he loved so, she had become a real favourite of his.

He taught her backgammon and canasta as well. But she beat him every time. He remembered taking the two of them up to Wrigley Road Street market one Sunday, where the two sisters got engrossed in looking at rather explicit birthday cards, mostly showing coloured men with large organs, and on marathon day, the three of them had gone for a boat trip up to Westminster Bridge. And she had become a frequent visitor with Mia. He had always appreciated her phoning him and reassuring him during the time of the original crisis and he genuinely enjoyed being in her company. She now had an affair going on with a guy called Dave. Mia was apprehensive about it because from what Harper said, it was more sexual than anything else.

A far cry from 'return unopened' he thought. She had a personal problem that she asked Charlie's advice on, and things like that did help him to think he was part of the family after all. Her sister Shirley was different to both of them, much deeper and more intense; she also was now very much involved with her boyfriend Ian. They both worked for Dom Air and consequently were always flying off somewhere exotic. Charlie's first remembrance of her had been unfortunate; he had driven down to the Gatwick Hilton to meet Mia for the evening. Harper was her cover and Charlie also met Eric for the first time.

He and Mia then went off together stopping for a meal in a bistro that he remembered from his Tracey's days. It gave him a strange feeling to be back there again; he thought to himself how much his life had changed, in the years between. He had waited all this time before the miracle of meeting his fantastic, fabulous girl, who had given him her love; he would never have foreseen that he could be so lucky. Mia was concerned that he didn't drink, as he had a long drive back to do, so they discovered Iceberg, a non-alcoholic wine for the first and last time. She was her usual lovely randy self that night, they had been parted for a week, and their coming together in the back of his car was a pleasure and joy to them both.

It was afterwards when they stopped to pick up Shirley from work that her mood changed; she really was rather standoffish to Charlie, which hurt and surprised him. Afterwards, of course, they became the best of friends. He had enjoyed that night particularly, how strange to be back in Horley again. The station he had used so many times, the roads and buildings he remembered so well. And which he had never expected to see again. It felt friendly and rather nice. And to be there with Mia and to be so happy at last, unbelievable.

In order to raise some extra money, Mia had started to use her sewing skills to full advantage. She had entirely of her own bat, gone into a local curtain shop and arranged with them for a supply of cushion covers. She had searched amongst her friends for any curtain work. And she collected up a mass of her children's old clothes and toys and sold them at a car boot sale in Chigwell. Charlie and his mother had supported her as much as possible on the day, but Mia had been the one doing all the work; her success filled him with admiration. She really was determined to prove her independence, even though she knew that she would never have to. Charlie would always look after her and support her and the girls; he supposed it was just her way of proving that she was no longer dependent on him.

Disaster struck at the end of May; Charlie was called to head office one Friday afternoon and made redundant. He was quite relieved because he had expected the sack. He left there and then, and decided to have the next four weeks off before sorting out what he was going to do. The following night, they were going to Wembley again; this time to see Elton John. Driving first to Twickenham to Ian's new flat, Mia told him how concerned Ian had been to hear of his redundancy. Charlie thought this was rather nice of him but completely unnecessary. The concert was outstanding; all their favourite songs, shouting out the choruses and standing, dancing in their seats the three sisters together were the knockout sight. Mia being the blondest stood out like a light, but they were all lovely and once again, Charlie found it hard to believe how lucky he had been.

On the way home, Mia took him to Garfunkel's for a late supper. A place she had known with Ramiro, away from her sisters. She seemed a little serious, but they had enjoyed a really fun evening. Together with his mother, they drove out to Coopersale to look at some new houses, stopping at a pub that Arthur and his mother had known in their early days. Charlie had great fun playing in the garden tree house with Olivia. He was making the most of his break and they took both the girls to Valentine Park, playing on the swings and climbing frames, and Olivia jumping on the bouncing castle. Charlie felt so content with 'his' little family this was his lifestyle now, what a fool he had been to miss out on so much pleasure for so long.

He thanked god for this late chance he had been given. He wasn't that keen on MacDonalds, but the lads liked it. His favourite family eating place in Buckhurst Hill gave the children hats, balloons, and special kiddies menus; things that he had never known existed now achieved so much importance to him, it seemed as if he and Mia were not just tender lovers, but closest friends and often just like two kids themselves.

Chapter 26
Full Circle

On the final week before going to Spain, Mia told him obviously she wanted to spend as much time with the girls as possible; she had arranged with her sisters that they would share the looking after duties. On Saturday night, they had one of their favourite Italian takeaways from the Belsit. Mia then gave a one-woman fashion show, trying on all the outfits that she had stored in his wardrobe. It was an immense turn-on to what her slip from outfit to outfit; she knew she was testing him, and she looked absolutely gorgeous. They had been nude sunbathing on the private roof and she already had a nice colour, she had told him that she had a mild case of thrush and that if he wanted any nookie in Spain, he had better get something for himself. He went to his doctors, where most embarrassing he found he had to see a new doctor instead, and she turned out to be a very attractive young girl.

They had been to Romford market together; strangely, she hadn't seemed that keen on him coming with her. There she bought a tube of fluorescent crepe material, and now she showed him what she had made for herself. The shortest, brightest mini dress she had ever worn, and the smallest bikini, both drove him nuts just watching her; he couldn't wait to get away with her, laughingly, she showed him the difficulty in wearing the dress without knickers, fine until she sat down when of course all was revealed. She said what he thought Aidan would say about that; Charlie said, "It's not Aidan, it's Victoria, who would have something to say."

Watching her reminded him of all the other lovely outfits he had seen her dressing and undressing in. His favourite office outfit, a long black skirt, and grey check jacket, her long yellow skirt—with matching shoes, with a floral jacket, her old ski jacket, her white dress with huge flowers on, which she often wore with a white jacket, her blue denim mini, her leggings, and grey jeans and his favourite short red boots; he remembered how she had carried a condom in one of those boots, tipping it out at the appropriate moment.

At the same time that Charlie had been transferred to Barkingside, Mia had been made redundant, but the firm had offered her some temporary show flat work in Chadwell Heath. Now she worked from 10.30 to 3.30 every Sunday. On this last Sunday, she called in from work but left early in the evening rather than stay as Charlie had expected. She had originally told him she would stay on Wednesday night, which he was looking forward to; now, she said she wanted to spend the night with the kids at Ian's flat. This meant that since they had long awaited tickets for Aspect of Love, which they hoped would be another Les Misérables for them, they would now have to meet separately in London in the evening, then take Mia back to Twickenham, drive back to Woodward, then Charlie would take the cases on the train to Gatwick and Mia would make her own way there and meet him.

At Mia's suggestion, Charlie's mum was coming to the theatre with them and had so been looking forward to it.

Now Mia's change of plans buggered up all the arrangements. Charlie was in a bad mood by the time they got there. Mia's attitude towards him for the past week had upset him over and over; she seemed cold and thoughtless, and he could not for the life of him figure out what was causing it. Their lovemaking had turned more into just sex sessions when Mia needed it, but he wasn't really worried; they both knew that if it didn't improve by itself, he could have treatment; it might even be fun trying it out together. But now in these last two weeks, it was almost as if she was withdrawing from him. He felt that in some indefinable way, she was deliberately pushing him to have a row with her. Even the prospect of this lovely evening at the theatre had seemed to be an intrusion to her and she was showing no excitement about the holiday.

Sitting in the Pizza House in Leicester Square with his mother, Charlie kept impatiently looking out of the window, sure that Mia would be late. Suddenly he saw her and his mood changed immediately; there she was in her best pink outfit, beautifully made up and right on time. A lump formed in his throat as he ran out to meet her; what was wrong with him, how could he ever doubt her he thought. The show was excellent, the music lovely, the theme that love will conquer everything was one that was most poignant to Charlie, but without that magical Les Miserable feeling between them, it was just a pleasant show—and dropping her off to Ian's flat without so much as a peck on the cheek, didn't help matters.

The next morning, he struggled up to Victoria with the cases on his own. Mia had changed the plan again, she wouldn't be at Victoria, and she would go straight to Gatwick. Ian offered to take her by car; eventually, he arrived and waited at the arranged spot. Instead of feeling over the moon that the two of them were actually going away together after all this time, he felt vaguely apprehensive; his happiness was tinged with doubts now, why and why had Mia been acting so coldly, what on earth was the matter between them, why was so carelessly hurting him so much and so often?

When she arrived, his fears evaporated; she was wearing her lovely white dress with the large flowers on; once again, they had made it. He hugged and kissed her, she responded to the kiss but was just limp in his arms. He purposefully raised her arms and put them around his waist himself, and she laughed as if to say sorry I forgot. The other four arrived shortly afterwards. Charlie told them he had just seen Cilla Black checking onto their flight, so they all had to go and gawped for themselves. Mia and Jordan's wife Michelle went to phone their kids and then they were into the departure lounge. Mia had not stopped for anything to eat, so Charlie bought her a large cooked breakfast; it turned out that none of the others had eaten either, and they descended like a flock of vultures, clearing the plate in seconds.

The two of them being the only smokers were relegated to the rear of the plane; it was of course their first flight together. Mia seemed happier by the hour and Charlie began to relax himself; this was the same trip she had done the previous August.

Aidan's apartment was only a couple of miles away from where she stayed, but for Charlie who had never liked Spain much anyway, it was entirely new. He had never had any desire to visit this area, but of course, he was happy to go absolutely anywhere with Mia. At Malaga, they had an amusing episode, Micky Dolenz the former Monkee pop star had also been on their flight. Charlie remembered playing poker against him at the Cromrellian Club back in the sixties; now here he was with a leather cowboy hat on, and fringed waistcoat, stopped by the customs men, and probably put on the next flight. They crammed into a four-seater hire car and had about an hour's drive in acute discomfort. Aidan's place was really lovely, spacious and cool, set in lovely gardens with a super pool, their room had twin beds and led onto a large balcony; they unpacked and settled in to enjoy themselves.

The mixture of friends worked like a charm. Mia hardly knew Jordan's wife Michelle, who she knew and liked from playschool. Aidan, she knew very well by now. He of course knew all her intimate details which gave them a good understanding of each other.

On their first night, they dined in the open-air restaurant by the beach, all drinking to excess. They decided to leave the car and walk back. Victoria was the most sober, which was just as well because they would have easily gotten lost in the state they were in. Charlie lagged behind on purpose; he was feeling most romantic in the moonlight, she however was oblivious to this, chatting and laughing to the others, in the end, he gave up the idea and caught them up. After a marathon of uphill shambles, they eventually arrived home and collapsed noisily around the pool. By the time they eventually got to bed, it was passing out time.

Charlie watched Mia for a time from his own bed; they hadn't even had a good night kiss, but if he was honest, he would have to agree that they were bottom drunk and exhausted. Rising late, they sunbathed around the pool all day; Mia beat both Jordan and Aidan at backgammon, much to their chagrin, and they taught Jordan how to play canasta. He as usual had absolutely no money on him at all, and trying to cash a Eurocheque. That evening, Charlie was determined to pay for the meal. Aidan had insisted on paying for everything so far.

They chose a restaurant in the town, spotting one of the so-called stars of Eastenders as they did so, Mia decided she would share paella with Charlie, but the meal was disappointing. Afterwards, they went for a walk and ended up playing ten-pin bowls. None of them had a clue, but Charlie somehow came from behind and just beat Jordan to win after another abortive effort to cash Jordan's cheque, they happily wandered their way back.

On Saturday, the others all went off shopping, this was really the first time Mia and Charlie had been alone since they arrived. They went up to the top-floor balcony and indulged in nude sunbathing. Mia didn't seem very communicative, so they read and lazed in the hot sunshine; there wasn't an atmosphere between them, rather Mia seemed preoccupied. Watching her stretched out, Charlie counted his blessings once again. How was it possible that this young gorgeous young girl could possibly have fallen for him?

He eyed her hungrily over and over, fixing a picture of every part of her body in his mind; slowly he aroused her, giving her a long gentle oral orgasm, enjoying her groans of pleasure when she was done. She dropped back to sleep again, but he didn't care; he knew she would give him his pleasure later. That night, they were going to a nightclub restaurant, so they all got dressed up at their best.

Tony Dalli the owner was an elderly Italian, who had once back in the days of black and white television had a hit single, now long forgotten, photos and posters of him were everywhere, and they had a table close to Cilla Blacks. The lovely carefree happy evening was only spoilt for Charlie once; he could not take his eyes off Mia. With her new tan, she looked mind-blowingly beautiful, turning every male head in the place, even though there were many more other lovely girls present. He leaned over to tell her how fabulous she looked and she snapped at him not to be silly and to stop embarrassing her in front of the others. Tony sang all the well-known romantic songs; the meal was excellent and the atmosphere lovely.

Afterwards, they went to Porto Bells, a very expensive ex-fishing village now jammed with luxury yachts and launches. Mia rang the girls and that seemed to make her happy again. They strolled around the harbour and then sat in a bar watching the local talent pass up and down endlessly. Charlie felt immense relief that the days when he might have had to be out there on the lookout for girls in the meat market were over. He had got his love; he would never need another; this time it had worked and continued to work, except for these last couple of weeks of doubts and his recent failures with her. And they would soon be worked out.

On Sunday, they again sunbathed around the pool, Mia by now had started topless; the other two girls declined. Sitting on her sunbed with her legs apart, her crutch within a couple of feet of Jordan's eye level, brought him the classic comment as he started mesmerised, "I don't know if I should be playing backgammon or snooker." The final night coincided with Charlie's 49th birthday, starting from midnight, not an event he was in any way looking forward to, but he had Mia's love of that he could be sure and so that also just like his redundancy became bearable what did it matter with Mia to inspire him.

The whole world was there to conquer. In the afternoon, Aidan and Victoria wanted some time to themselves, so the other four borrowed the car, and with Charlie driving, made their way down the route of death, to Banana Beach, where there was a lovely friendly atmosphere, mostly young people, with a line rock group, stalls and bars. There were a multitude of books on display of all shapes and sizes, but Charlie really only had eyes for Mia. She didn't have the biggest bust in the world, but to him, they were amongst the nicest he had ever known. He loved the shape and the firmness of them, remarkable in a girl who had breastfed two babies, and the first time he had seen her nipples, he had come out in goose pimples. He had always had a thing about the shape and size of nipples rather than breasts themselves and he had been disappointed on many occasions—Mia's were perfect and then he discovered they were her most erogenous zone, and indeed essential to her satisfaction, he had been in seventh heaven.

Way back at the beginning of their love, she had mentioned getting a bright pink self-adhesive plastic 'shell' bikini bottom. He had then had a most erotic dream of walking hand in hand with her along, some foreign beach. They had laughed about it then because it had seemed impossible. Now he was to accomplish one more little fantasy. It wasn't plastic, it wasn't bright pink, but it was peach, and it was very small and she looked ravishing.

That night, they looked for somewhere nice to celebrate the birthday boy. Playing pool with Jordan, Charlie to his astonishment beat him. He had also won £30 playing canasta with him. It seemed that he was indeed on a lucky roll, what with the free holiday, as well, he had been thinking quite hard about what to do next for a living. If this lucky streak continued, he might even open an office of his own again. If only Mia wasn't determined to go to her parents, they could do it together; he would make her an equal partner, just like had planned in the beginning, if only this coldness of hers could be sorted. How much easier it would be for the girls if they could stay at their schools and keep their friends, all the other plans could come later, and all these thoughts were pouring through his head as they enjoyed the evening.

They all got well plastered as if was the last night. Dining in a Lebanese open-air restaurant, they toasted his health at midnight, filled with love, emotion and wine, and in the company of his close friends, Charlie misread the occasion. Mia had been happy and laughing all evening; he felt there could be no better time or company to celebrate Mia and his future with. Looking lovingly at her, he was about to reply to their toasts to him, by asking them to drink to Mia and himself. She was free now, at last, he soon would be. She somehow sensed exactly what he was about to propose and snapped at him, "No, Charlie, this is not the time for this."

He felt as if she had physically stabbed him; the others noticed nothing, and the party continued; he was suddenly stone-cold sober. Withdrawing into himself as the others got more and more intoxicated, he thought back to an incident earlier in the afternoon, buying two giant ice-cream sundaes, just like a couple of kids when the conversation turned to bimbos. Never in a million years would anyone see Mia as Charlie's bimbo, but she seemed somehow to take it personally; she had certainly never let the age difference affect them either in public or in private when he had raised the subject initially, she had said it only meant she regretted the 20 years they could never have together, why would she now start to think otherwise.

As they left the restaurant, the others all in very high spirits, he tried not to let his hurt show. Someone had filled the ornamental ponds and fountains with foam.

Aidan jumped into one; he bought a leather whip from a native and since Mia owed Jordan several pounds from losing at canasta, she agreed to be 'whipped' in public if full and final settlement. Aidan had already given a demonstration of mooning in the foam. Mia now hiked up her mini dress so that she could be 'beaten' in public. Much to the glee of the other diners and passers-by running around the corner, they came across a large, parked motorbike, Jenny and Mia then laid across the seat suggestively, Jordan pulled down their knickers, hoisted up their skirts and whipped them again for the camera. Staggering back to their own pool, Aidan and Victoria were splashing about romantically.

Mia decided she wanted to tease him by pulling off his bathing trunks, knowing that this would immediately give him the excuse to reciprocate; she jumped out of her own first; it was difficult to decide which one was squealing the loudest when Aidan discovered that he had been beaten to it.

Eventually, they went to their respective bedrooms, and Mia for whatever reason, maybe because it was their last night or Charlie's birthday, or just that she was randy, made it quite obvious that tonight was the night, rolling together naked on the marble floor, they were soon very much engrossed in each other. The number of times she had given him oral intercourse could be counted on one hand, not because she was averse like it with him, or it was a hangover from Ramiro's days; he had usually said to her 'anyone would think it was my birthday'; tonight it was. They ended up on the balcony and there in the warm Spanish night, bathed in moonlight, he matched her right up until the last moment, he could feel the climax mounting in her and he could certainly hear the reaction he was getting; she was on top faster and harder than ever before; he was well aware that the others upstairs could not fail to hear them and this gave him even more endurance. He finished seconds only before her and knew without any doubt that this time there was no faking or failure; she was there at the biggest climax he had ever given her when suddenly inches from their bodies, someone closed the lounge door.

It was gone, snatched away at the very moment of victory. Both of them were too exhausted to try again. Love had very little to do with it, but Charlie had proved once and for all that he could match her even at this new wild level of hers. The next day was a misery; Charlie hated having to take her back. He wanted to stay away with her as long as possible; she wanted to get back as quickly as possible, and it was instead of being a lovely birthday for him, and absolute torment, the flight home was unbearable, whatever form of conversation he tried to interest her in failed. They hardly spoke, and his doubts and fears gnawed away inside. He could actually feel once more, the whole thing slipping away; this time, it was him it was slipping from, not the other way round as had felt with Tracey.

She was leaving them at the airport; Ian again was picking her up, and since he may have the girls with him, Charlie should not wait and see her off even. She told him that she had to make up time with the girls now and wouldn't see much of him for the rest of the week. He held her almost desperately and the fierceness of his goodbye kiss startled her. But deep down, he had this dreadful feeling of losing her, and it was shattering him there and then. Hurt and dismayed, he once again parted from her and went home alone, what a birthday!

Chapter 27
The Last Rites

He spent the next few days sorting out all his plans for a business; one by one, they failed to materialise. All the prospects he had thought about when he didn't need to, now failed to work once he did need them. He did receive an agreement to open a new office jointly as an agency and a letting business from one of his contacts, but with the market stone dead now, the actual cost would be suicidal. The premises were just up the road, ideally situated, and at any time, he would have taken the chance gladly, but what was the point of tying himself down in Woodward with Mia going to Sussex? He decided instead to apply himself to working for someone else again or maybe re-financing and extending his present hotel. If he was going to stay in Woodward for any length of time, that would make sense, whatever else he did, he knew that he had to bring matters to a head with Mia, they couldn't go on like this. It was literally tearing holes in him, and what sort of state must she be in, to be acting so cruelly, it had to be resolved.

She eventually arrived late on Saturday evening, happy to chat with his mother about the children, and the holiday; she mentioned that she had been to a school quiz night with

Jordan and Michelle. Charlie had known nothing about it, but would have loved to join in; he took her up to his bedroom, where they finished recording Evita for her. His birthday present she had ordered had finally arrived on the 'secret' day out with his mother; she had driven all the way back to the shop in Windsor, just to buy the special soldiers she knew he wanted. The shop had been closed so she had to write off for them and they had been late. When he saw the enormous trouble she had been to just for his pleasure, he became even more sure of her real feelings for him and decided that now was the moment to sort things between them again. He loved her more dearly than ever they had to make it work.

They had come such a long way together in nearly two years. Picking his words carefully, he began, warning her gently that they couldn't go on like they were. Mia's most frustrating habit was the fact that whenever she had to give an answer to a direct question, she would pause whilst she weighed up each word for anything up to 30 seconds. This time however she came straight out with the answers as if she had been preparing them ready. "No," she said.

They couldn't go on at all; they sat on the bed, she cried softly and told him how she hated to hurt him, how she was so sorry to let him down, but now she had to finish their relationship. The words washed over him; he could not believe what he was hearing. She said that he no longer physically attracted her, and his failures to satisfy her had made her too frustrated to continue. "I want to finish so that I don't do to you, what we did to Ramiro," she said, and she implied that it was finally the age difference that had been insurmountable for her. He begged her to reconsider, how could she just go without at least them trying?

She said that she knew he could sort out the actual sexual performance, but that it would only peak for a while, delaying the inevitable. He told her that he just could not accept it there and then; it was impossible to break the ties just like that. He tried to remind her of just how much she would be giving up, the phoning, the trust, the interests, the security, safety for the girls, the company, the understanding. She was impervious to all his persuasions. She would not spend even this one last night with him; she was gone.

Chapter 28
No Title

There was, of course, no sleep that night; his worst nightmare was facing him.

He could not, would not accept that either of them could give up just like that, the total closeness they had enjoyed for so many months, her reliance on him, how did she suddenly think she could manage without him? He had asked her why in heaven's name she hadn't let them have a break in March when they needed it. She had replied that at that time she didn't think she could live without him, her words kept coming back to him, so how could she now suddenly manage?

Did she think the divorce was the end of her problems? What about Charlotte, the biggest problem of all was still to come with her, hadn't he proved over and over that he would be able to help her adjust, wasn't that what he had just spent two years carefully preparing? Had Mia thought this out, had she even thought of it at all? The sheer panic at the very thought of a life without Mia and the girls made him feel sick and shaky. Where had he failed?

What was the main fault? Find it and work on putting it right, face the fact that they would after all have to try to break for a while, just how he would get through that break, he had no idea, but once again, he would have to fight. This time for his very life. Obviously, he must consult his specialist immediately, once they implemented his necessary improvements, Mia would be satisfied again. Hadn't she thanked him and said all their times had been wonderful, of course, they had. Nothing in either of their lives would even come close to the feelings they had enjoyed. He should know, hadn't he waited so long himself to find out? He had told her that she should stop phoning him, otherwise, every time it rang, he would think it was her, that in itself would make her stop and think, she needed the reassurance of speaking on the phone all the time, didn't she?

He had also asked her to take all her personal belongings away. He loved having them around him but now they would be a constant reminder that he couldn't bear, and that also was something she hadn't considered, where else could she store them?

He couldn't settle down, of course, he felt dreadful, but his instincts had never yet let him down; of course, it was going to be rough, but defeat in this was unthinkable, between the two of them, they must be able to talk it out. On Sunday, he forced himself to stay away from her show flat. It was a lovely sunny day, but he didn't take her deck chair or portable TV over to her. Throughout the day, his other problems piled up on him.

His mother's health was now in major concern; she had been for further tests and it was confirmed that she had a thrombosis condition in her leg, which required a quick hospital admission. Mia said all along that she would help him, when his mother had the operation, now of course, he would somehow manage alone. He must also find another job quickly. The repayments for Kat's loan had to be found each month, or his savings would fritter away, but above all, there was Mia. He couldn't concentrate on anything for more than half an hour without thought of her, and how to get her back to being happy again, flooded in on him.

On Monday morning, as he was leaving the video shop, he bumped into her, ringing someone from the corner phone booth, he saw Ollie first and she came running over to his car happily.

Mia laughed and smiled at him as if there was nothing changed; his throat went dry; he felt nauseous, and she looked as if she didn't have a care in the world. The rest of the week dragged by. He went to his specialist; it was confirmed again that even if he was useless, which he certainly wasn't the techniques available would be more than enough to make any girl happy.

They explained how much easier it would be if Mia would attend with him; from his as honest as possible description, they diagnosed her as 'Orgasmastic,' he didn't give a damn what name they called it; to him, it was a lovely gift, something to rejoice in, but even if they had proved she was a nymphomaniac, it wouldn't have made any difference. In fact, he would have found that quite undesirable. He had known a couple when he was younger, to whom constant sex was a tearing need, but one without pleasure. Mia was nothing like that, she needed the pleasure but she also enjoyed giving it just as much. He wondered again just how much her years with Ramiro had hardened her, what a pig he was, how could he have treated her like a whore, the mother of his children, what sort of mind would take photos and videos of his own wife he had.

Obviously, he had absolutely no respect for her at all, but now handicapped it had made Charlie follow him. There was, of course, a world of difference between crudeness and rudeness, but in the physical side of sex acts, where Charlie would have loved to be more expressive with her and who was naturally rude himself, he had been totally handicapped with Mia. Wasn't it the fact that Ramiro used her just for his own pleasure, that had drawn her to Charlie in the first place?

The author passed away in December 2018. His wife has found the manuscript among his collectables and other books few months later. She could not bring herself to read it – it took a few months, and then more months to type it up and bring it to share the story with the world.